"*Danki* for your help today, Esther."

"I'm glad you're my friend. You've been my friend since we were *kinder*, and I hope you'll be my friend for the rest of our lives." She put her hand out and clasped his. Giving it a squeeze, she started to release it and turn away.

Nathaniel's fingers closed over hers, keeping her where she stood. She couldn't look away from his eyes. She longed to discover what he was thinking.

Suddenly she stiffened. What was she thinking? Hadn't she decided she needed to make sure he knew friendship was all they should share? She drew her arm away, and, after a moment's hesitation, he lifted his fingers from hers.

"*Ja*," he said. "I'm glad, too, we're always going to be friends. It's for the best."

"For us and for Jacob."

"Of course for Jacob, too." A cool smile settled on his lips. "That's what I meant."

"I know." She took another step away. She couldn't remember ever being less than honest with Nathaniel before. But it was for his own *gut*.

She had to believe that, but she hadn't guessed facing the truth would be so painful.

Jo Ann Brown has always loved stories with happy-ever-after endings. A former military officer, she is thrilled to have the chance to write stories about people falling in love. She is also a photographer, and she travels with her husband of more than thirty years to places where she can snap pictures. They live in Nevada with three children and a spoiled cat. Drop her a note at joannbrownbooks.com.

Books by Jo Ann Brown

Love Inspired

Amish Hearts

Amish Homecoming
An Amish Match
His Amish Sweetheart

Love Inspired Historical

Matchmaking Babies

Promise of a Family
Family in the Making
Her Longed-For Family

Sanctuary Bay

The Dutiful Daughter
A Hero for Christmas
A Bride for the Baron

His Amish
Sweetheart

Jo Ann Brown

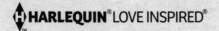

HARLEQUIN® LOVE INSPIRED®

Recycling programs for this product may not exist in your area.

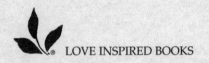

LOVE INSPIRED BOOKS

ISBN-13: 978-0-373-71975-4

His Amish Sweetheart

www.Harlequin.com

Printed in U.S.A.

For if thou altogether holdest thy peace at this time, then shall there enlargement and deliverance arise to the Jews from another place; but thou and thy father's house shall be destroyed: and who knoweth whether thou art come to the kingdom for such a time as this?
—*Esther* 4:14

For John Jakaitis
Thank you for helping us find our way home.

Chapter One

Paradise Springs
Lancaster County, Pennsylvania

Esther Stoltzfus balanced the softball bat on her shoulder. Keeping her eye on the boy getting ready to pitch the ball, she smiled. Did her scholars guess that recess, when the October weather was perfect for playing outside, was her favorite part of the day, too? The *kinder* probably couldn't imagine their teacher liked to play ball as much as they did.

This was her third year teaching on her own. Seeing understanding in a *kind*'s eyes when the scholar finally grasped an elusive concept delighted her. She loved spending time with the *kinder*.

Her family had recently begun dropping hints she should be walking out with some young man. Her older brothers didn't know that, until eight months ago, she'd been walking out—and sneaking out for some forbidden buggy racing—with Alvin Lee Peachy. Probably because none of them could have imagined their little sister having such an outrageous suitor. Alvin Lee pushed the boundaries of the *Ordnung*, and there were rumors he intended to jump the fence and join the *Englisch* world. Would she have gone with him if he'd asked? She didn't know, and she never would because when she began to worry about his racing buggies and fast life, he'd dumped her and started courting Luella Hartz. In one moment, she'd lost the man she loved and her *gut* friend.

She'd learned her lesson. A life of adventure and daring wasn't for her. From now on, she wasn't going to risk her heart unless she knew, without a doubt, it was safe. She wouldn't consider spending time with a guy who wasn't as serious and stolid as a bishop.

As she gave a practice swing and the *kinder* urged her on excitedly, she glanced at her assistant teacher, Neva Fry, who was playing first base. Neva, almost two years younger than Esther, was learning what she needed so she could take over a school of her own.

Esther grinned in anticipation of the next play. The ball came in a soft arc, and she swung the bat. Not with all her strength. Some of the outfielders were barely six years old, and she didn't want to chance them getting hurt by a line drive.

The *kinder* behind her cheered while the ones in the field shouted to each other to catch the lazy fly ball. She sped to first base, a large stone set in place by the *daeds* who had helped build the school years ago. Her black sneaker skidded as she touched the stone with one foot and turned to head toward second. Seeing one of the older boys catch the ball, she slowed and clapped her hands.

"Well done, Jay!" she called.

With a wide grin, the boy who, at fourteen, was in his final year at the school, gave her a thumbs-up.

Smiling, she knew she should be grateful Alvin Lee hadn't proposed. She wasn't ready to give up teaching. She wanted a husband and a home and *kinder* of her own, but not until she met the right man. One who didn't whoop at the idea of danger. One she would have described as predictable a few months ago. Now that safe, dependable guy sounded like a dream come true. Well, maybe not a dream, but definitely not a nightmare.

Checking to make sure her *kapp* was straight, Esther smoothed the apron over her dress, which was her favorite shade of rose. She'd selected it and a black apron in the style the *Englischers* called a pinafore when she saw the day would be perfect for playing softball. She held up her hands, and Jay threw her the ball. She caught it easily.

Before she could tell the scholars it was time to go in for afternoon lessons, several began to chant, "One more inning! One more inning!"

Esther hesitated, knowing how few sunny, warm days remained before winter. The *kinder* had worked hard during the morning, and she hadn't had to scold any of them for not paying attention. Not even Jacob Fisher.

She glanced at the small, white schoolhouse. As she expected, the eight-year-old with a cowlick that made a black exclamation point at his crown sat alone on the porch. She invited him to play each day, and each day he resisted. She wished she could find a way to break through the walls Jacob had raised, walls around himself, walls to keep pain at bay.

She closed her eyes as she recalled what she'd been told by Jacob's elderly *onkel*, who was raising him. Jacob had been with his parents, walking home from visiting a neighbor, when they were struck by a drunk driver.

The boy had been thrown onto the shoulder. When he regained consciousness, he'd discovered his parents injured by the side of the road. No one, other than Jacob and God, knew if they spoke final words to him, but he'd watched them draw their last breaths. The trial for the hit-and-run driver had added to the boy's trauma, though he hadn't had to testify and the Amish community tried to shield him.

Now he was shattered, taking insult at every turn and exploding with anger. Or else he said nothing and squirmed until he couldn't sit any longer and had to wander around the room. Working with his *onkel*, Titus Fisher, she tried to make school as comfortable for Jacob as possible.

She'd used many things she hoped would help—art projects, story writing, extra assistance with his studies, though the boy was very intelligent in spite of his inability to complete many of his lessons. She'd failed at every turn to draw him out from behind those walls he'd raised around himself. She realized she must find another way to reach him because she wasn't helping him by cajoling him in front of the other *kinder*. So now, she lifted him up in prayer. Those wouldn't fail, but God worked on His own time. He must have a reason for not yet bringing healing to Jacob's young heart.

Or hers.

She chided herself. Losing a suitor didn't compare with losing one's parents, but her heart refused to stop hurting.

"All right," she said, smiling at the rest of the scholars because she didn't want anyone to know what she was thinking. She'd gotten *gut* at hiding the truth. "One more inning, but you need to work extra hard this afternoon."

Heads nodded eagerly. Bouncing the ball in her right hand, she tossed it to the pitcher and took her place in center field where she could help the other outfielders, seven-year-old Olen and Freda who was ten.

The batter swung at the first three pitches and struck out. The next batter kept hitting foul balls, which sent the *kinder* chasing them. Suddenly a loud thwack announced a boy had connected with the ball.

It headed right for Esther. She backpedaled two steps. A quick glance behind her assured she could go a little farther before she'd fall down the hill. Shouts warned her the runner was already on his way to second base.

She reached to catch the ball. Her right foot caught a slippery patch of grass, and she lost her balance. She windmilled her arms, fighting to stay on her feet, but it was impossible. She dropped backward—and hit a solid chest. Strong arms kept her from ending up on her bottom. She grasped the arms as her feet continued to slide.

The ball fell at her feet. Pulling herself out of the arms, she scooped the ball up and threw it to second base. But it was too late. The run had already scored.

Behind her, a deep laugh brushed the small hairs curling at her nape beneath her *kapp*. Heat scored Esther's face as she realized she'd tumbled into a man's arms.

Her gaze had to rise to meet his, though he stood below her on the hill. He must be more than six feet tall, like her brothers, but he wasn't one of her brothers. The *gut*-looking man was a few years older than she was. No beard softened the firm line of his jaw. Beneath his straw hat, his brown eyes crinkled with his laugh.

"You haven't changed a bit, Esther Stoltzfus!" he said with another chuckle. "Still willing to risk life and limb to get the ball."

He knew her? Who was he?

Her eyes widened. She recognized the twinkle in those dark eyes. Black hair dropped across his forehead, and he pushed it aside carelessly. Like a clap of thunder, realization came as she remembered the boy who had made that exact motion. She looked more closely and saw the small scar beneath his right eye…just like the one on the face of a boy she'd once considered her very best friend.

"Nate Zook?" she asked, not able to believe her own question.

"Ja." His voice was much deeper than when she'd last heard it. "Though I go by Nathaniel now."

When she'd last seen him, he'd been…ten or eleven? She'd been eight. Before his family moved away, she and Nate, along with Micah and Daniel, her twin brothers, had spent most days together. Then, one day, the Zooks were gone. Her brothers had been astonished when they rode their scooters to Nate's house and discovered it was empty. When her *mamm* said the family had moved to Indiana in search of a better life, she wondered if it'd been as much a surprise for Nate as for her and her brothers.

She'd gone with Daniel and Micah to play at his grandparents' farm in a neighboring district when he visited the next summer, but she shouldn't have. She'd accepted a dare from a friend to hold Nate's hand. She couldn't remember which friend it'd been, but at the time she'd been excited to do something audacious. She'd embarrassed herself by following through and gripping his hand so tightly he winced and made it worse by telling him that she planned to marry him when they grew up. He hadn't come back the following summer. She'd been grateful she didn't have to face him after her silliness, and miserable because she missed him.

That was in the past. Here stood Nate—Nathaniel—Zook again, a grown man who'd arrived in time to keep her from falling down the hill.

She should say something. Several *kinder* came to stand beside her, curious about what was going on. She needed to show she wasn't that silly little girl any longer, but all that came out was, "What are you doing in Paradise Springs?"

He opened his mouth to answer. Whatever he was about to say was drowned out by a shriek from the schoolhouse.

Esther whirled and gasped when she saw two boys on the ground, fists flying. She ran to stop the fight. Finding out why Nathaniel had returned to Paradise Springs after more than a decade would have to wait. But not too long, because she was really curious why he'd come back now.

Nathaniel Zook stared after Esther as she raced across the grass, her apron flapping on her skirt. Years ago, she'd been able to outrun him and her brothers, though they were almost five years older than she was. She'd been much shorter then, and her knees, which were now properly concealed beneath her dress, had been covered with scrapes. Her bright eyes were as blue, and their steady gaze contained the same strength.

He looked past her to where two boys were rolling on the grass. Should he help? One of the boys in the fight was nearly as big as Esther was.

"Oh, Jacob Fisher! He keeps picking fights," said a girl with a sigh.

"Or dropping books on the floor or throwing papers

around." A boy shook his head. "He wants attention. That's what my *mamm* says."

Nathaniel didn't wait to listen to any more because when Esther bent to try to put a halt to the fight, a fist almost struck her. He crossed the yard and pushed past the gawking *kinder*. A blow to Esther's middle knocked her back a couple of steps. Again he caught her and steadied her, then he grasped both boys by their suspenders and tugged them apart.

The shorter boy struggled to get away, his brown eyes snapping with fury. Flinging his fists out wildly, he almost connected with the taller boy's chin.

Shoving them away from each other, Nathaniel said, "Enough. If you can't honestly tell each other you're sorry for acting foolishly, at least shake hands."

"I'm not shaking hands with him!" The taller boy was panting, and blood dripped from the left corner of his mouth. "He'll jump me again for no reason."

The shorter boy puffed up like a snake about to strike. "You called me a—"

"Enough," Nathaniel repeated as he kept a tight hold on their suspenders. "What's been said was said. What's been done has been done. It's over. Let it go."

The glowers the boys gave him warned Nathaniel that he was wasting his breath.

"Benny," ordered Esther, "go and wash up. Jacob, wait on the porch for me. We need to talk." She gestured toward a younger woman who'd been staring wide-eyed at the battling boys. "Neva, take the other scholars inside please."

Astonished by how serene her voice was and how quickly the boys turned to obey after scowling at each other again, Nathaniel waited while the *kinder* followed

Neva into the school. He knew Esther would want to get back to her job, as well. Since he'd returned to Paradise Springs, he'd heard over and over what a devoted teacher Esther Stoltzfus was. Well, his visit should be a short one because all he needed was for her to say a quick *ja*.

First, however, he had to ask, "Are you okay, Esther?"

"I'm fine." She adjusted her *kapp*, which had come loose in the melee. Her golden-brown hair glistened through the translucent white organdy of her heart-shaped *kapp*. Her dress was a charming dark pink almost the same color as her cheeks. The flush nearly absorbed her freckles. There weren't as many as the last time he'd seen her more than a decade ago.

Back then, she and her twin brothers had been his best friends. In some ways, he'd been closer to her than her brothers. Micah and Daniel were twins, and they had a special bond. He and Esther had often found themselves on one team while her brothers took the other side, whether playing ball or having races or embarking on some adventure. She hadn't been one of those girly girls who worried about getting her clothes dirty or if her hair was mussed. She played to win, though she was younger than the rest of them. He'd never met another girl like her, a girl who was, as his *daed* had described her, not afraid to be one of the boys.

"Are you sure?" he asked. "You got hit pretty hard."

"I'm fine." Her blue eyes regarded him with curiosity. "When did you return to Paradise Springs?"

"Almost a month ago. I've inherited my grandparents' farm on the other side of the village."

"I'm sorry, Nat—Nathaniel. I should have remembered that they'd passed away in the spring. You must miss them."

"Ja," he said, though the years that had gone by since the last time he'd seen them left them as little more than childhood memories. Except for one visit to Paradise Springs the first year after the move, his life had been in Elkhart County, Indiana.

From beyond the school he heard the rattle of equipment and smelled the unmistakable scent of greenery and disturbed earth. Next year at this time, God willing, he'd be chopping his own corn into silage to feed his animals over the winter. He couldn't wait. At last, he had the job he'd always wanted: farmer. He wouldn't have had the opportunity in Indiana. There it was intended, in Amish tradition, that his younger brother would inherit the family's five acres. Nathaniel had assumed he, like his *daed,* would spend his life working in an *Englisch* factory building RVs.

Those plans had changed when word came that his Zook grandparents' farm in Paradise Springs was now his. A dream come true. Along with the surprising menagerie his *grossdawdi* and his *grossmammi* had collected in their final years. He'd been astonished not to find dairy cows when he arrived. Instead, there were about thirty-five alpacas, one of the oddest looking animals he'd ever seen. They resembled a combination of a poodle and a llama, especially at this time of year when their wool was thickening. In addition, on the farm were two mules, a buggy horse and more chickens than he could count. He was familiar with horses, mules and chickens, but he had a lot to learn about alpacas, which was the reason he'd come to the school today.

He was determined to make the farm a success so he wouldn't have to sell it. For the first time in far too many years, he felt alive with possibilities.

"How can I help you?" Esther asked, as if he'd spoken aloud. "Are you here to enroll a *kind* in school?"

Years of practice kept him from revealing how her simple question drove a shaft through his heart. She couldn't guess how much that question hurt him, and he didn't have time to wallow in thoughts of how, because of a childhood illness, he most likely could never be a *daed*. He'd never enjoy the simple act of coming to a school to arrange for his son or daughter to attend.

He was alive and well. For that he was grateful, and he needed to let the feelings of failure go. Otherwise, he was dismissing God's gift of life as worthless. That he'd never do.

Instead he needed to concentrate on why he'd visited the school this afternoon. After asking around the area, he'd learned of only one person who was familiar with how to raise alpacas.

Esther Stoltzfus.

"No, I'm here for a different reason." He managed a smile. "One I think you'll find interesting."

"I'd like to talk, Nathaniel, but—" She glanced at the older boy, the one she'd called Benny. He stood by the well beyond the schoolhouse and was washing his hands and face. Jacob sat on the porch. He was trembling in the wake of the fight and rocking his feet against the latticework. It made a dull thud each time his bare heels struck it. "I'm going to have to ask you to excuse me. *Danki* for pulling the boys apart."

"The little guy doesn't look more than about six years old."

"Jacob is eight. He's small for his age, but he has the heart of a lion."

"But far less common sense if he fights boys twice his age."

"Benny is fourteen."

"Close enough."

She nodded with another sigh. "Yet you saw who ended up battered and bloody. Jacob doesn't have a mark on him."

"Quite a feat!"

"Really?" She frowned. "Think what a greater feat it would have been if Jacob had turned the other cheek and walked away from Benny. It's the lesson we need to take to heart."

"For a young boy, it's hard to remember. We have to learn things the hard way, it seems." He gave her a lopsided grin, but she wouldn't meet his eyes. She acted flustered. Why? She'd put a stop to the fight as quickly as she could. "Like the time your brothers and I got too close to a hive and got stung. I guess that's what people mean by a painful lesson."

"Most lessons are."

"Well, it was a *very* painful one." He hurried on before she could leave. "I've heard you used to raise alpacas."

"Just a pair. Are you planning to raise them on your grandparents' farm?"

"Not planning. They're already there. Apparently my *grossmammi* fell in love with the creatures and decided to buy some when she and my *grossdawdi* stopped milking. I don't know the first thing about alpacas, other than how to feed them. I was hoping you could share what you learned." He didn't add that if he couldn't figure out a way to use the animals to make money, he'd have to sell them and probably the farm itself next spring.

When she glanced at the school again, he said, "Not right now, of course."

"I'd like to help, but I don't have a lot of time."

"I won't need a lot of your time. Just enough to point me in the right direction."

She hesitated.

He could tell she didn't want to tell him no, but her mind was focused on the *kinder* now. Maybe he should leave and come back again, but he didn't have time to wait. The farm was more deeply in debt than he'd guessed before he came to Paradise Springs. He hadn't guessed his grandparents had spent so wildly on buying the animals that they had to borrow money for keeping them. Few plain folks their age took out a loan because it could become a burden on the next generation. Now it was his responsibility to repay it.

Inspiration struck when he looked from her to the naughty boys. It was a long shot, but he'd suggest anything if there was a chance to save his family's farm.

"Bring your scholars to see the alpacas," he said. "I can ask my questions, and so can they. You can answer them for all of us. It'll be fun for them. Remember how we liked a break from schoolwork? They would, too, I'm sure."

She didn't reply for a long minute, then nodded. "They probably would be really interested."

He grinned. "Why don't I drive my flatbed wagon over here? I can give the *kinder* a ride on it both ways."

"*Gut.* Let me know which day works best for you, and I'll tell the parents we're going there. Some of them may want to join us."

"We'll make an adventure out of it, like when we were *kinder.*"

Color flashed up her face before vanishing, leaving her paler than before.

"Was iss letz?" he asked.

"Nothing is wrong," she replied so hastily he guessed she wasn't being honest. "I—"

A shout came from the porch where the bigger boy was walking past Jacob. The younger boy was on his feet, his fists clenched again.

She ran toward them, calling over her shoulder, "We'll have to talk about this later."

"I'll come over tonight. We'll talk then."

Nathaniel wondered if she'd heard him because she was already steering the boys into the school. Her soft voice reached him. Not the words, but the gently chiding tone. He guessed she was reminding them that they needed to settle their disputes without violence. He wondered if they'd listen and what she'd have to do if they didn't heed her.

As she closed the door, she looked at him and mouthed, *See you tonight.*

"Gut!" he said as he walked to where he'd left his wagon on the road. He smiled. He'd been wanting to stop by the Stoltzfus farm, so her invitation offered the perfect excuse. It would be a fun evening, and for the first time since he'd seen the alpacas, he dared to believe that with what Esther could teach him about the odd creatures, he might be able to make a go of the farm.

Chapter Two

The Stoltzfus family farm was an easy walk from the school. Esther went across a field, along two different country roads, and then up the long lane to the only house she'd ever lived in. She'd been born there. Her *daed* had been as well, and his *daed* before him.

After *Daed* had passed away, her *mamm* had moved into the attached *dawdi haus* while Esther managed the main house. She'd hand over those duties when her older brother Ezra married, which she guessed would be before October was over, because he spent every bit of his free time with their neighbor Leah Beiler. Their wedding day was sure to be a joyous one.

Though she never would have admitted it, Esther was looking forward to giving the responsibilities of a household with five bachelor brothers to Leah. Even with one of her older brothers married, another widowed and her older sister off tending a family of her own, the housework was never-ending. Esther enjoyed cooking and keeping the house neat, but she was tired of mending a mountain of work clothes while trying to prepare lesson plans for the next day. Her brothers worked hard, whether on the farm or in construction or at the grocery store, and their clothes reflected that. She and *Mamm* never caught up.

Everything in her life had been in proper order...until Nathaniel Zook came to her school that afternoon. She was amazed she hadn't heard he was in Paradise Springs. If she'd known, maybe she'd have been better prepared. He'd grown up, but it didn't sound as if he'd changed. He still liked adventures if he intended to keep alpacas instead of the usual cows or sheep or goats on his farm. That made him a man she needed to steer clear of, so she could avoid the mistakes she'd made with Alvin Lee.

But how could she turn her back on helping him? It was the Amish way to give assistance when it was requested. She couldn't mess up Nathaniel's life because she was appalled by how she'd nearly ruined her own by chasing excitement.

His suggestion that she bring the scholars to his farm would focus attention on the *kinder*. She'd give them a fun day while they learned about something new, something that might be of use to them in the future. Who could guess now which one of them would someday have alpacas of his or her own?

That thought eased her disquiet enough that Esther could admire the trees in the front yard. They displayed their autumnal glory. Dried leaves were already skittering across the ground on the gentle breeze. Ezra's Brown Swiss cows grazed near the white barn. The sun was heading for the horizon, a sure sign milking would start soon. Dinner for her hungry brothers needed to be on the table by the time chores were done and the barn tidied up for the night.

When she entered the comfortable kitchen with its

pale blue walls and dark wood cabinets, Esther was surprised to see her twin brothers there. They were almost five years older than she was, and they'd teased her, when they were *kinder*, of being an afterthought. She'd fired back with jests of her own, and they'd spent their childhoods laughing. No one took offense while they'd been climbing trees, fishing in the creek and doing tasks to help keep the farm and the house running.

Her twin brothers weren't identical. Daniel had a cleft in his chin and Micah didn't. There were other differences in the way they talked and how they used their hands to emphasize words. Micah asserted he was a half inch taller than his twin, but Esther couldn't see it. They were unusual in one important way—they didn't share a birthday. Micah had been born ten minutes before midnight, and Daniel a half hour later, a fact Micah never allowed his "baby" brother to forget.

Both twins had a glass of milk in one hand and a stack of snickerdoodles in the other. Their bare feet stuck out from where they sat at the large table in the middle of the kitchen.

"You're home early," she said as she hung her bonnet and satchel on pegs by the back door. The twins' straw hats hung among the empty pegs, which would all be in use by the time the family sat down for dinner.

"We're finished at the project in Lititz," Daniel said. He was a carpenter, as was Micah, but the older twin specialized in building windmills and installing solar panels. However, the two men were equally skilled with a hammer. "Time to hand it over to the electricians and plumbers. Micah already went over what needed to be done to connect the roof panels to the main electrical box."

"You've been working on that house a long time," she said as she opened the refrigerator door and took out the leftover ham she planned to reheat for dinner. "It must be a big one."

"You know how *Englischers* are." Micah chuckled. "They move out to Lancaster County to live the simple life and then decide they need lots of gadgets and rooms to store them in. This house has a real movie theater."

She began cutting the ham into thick slices. "You're joking."

"Would we do that?" Daniel asked with fake innocence before he took the final bite of his last cookie.

"Ja."

"Ja," echoed Micah, folding his arms on the table. "We're being honest. The house is as big as our barn."

Esther tried to imagine why anyone would need a house that size, but she couldn't. At one point, there had been eleven of them living in the Stoltzfus farmhouse along with her grandparents in the small *dawdi haus*, and there had been plenty of room.

Daniel stretched before he yawned. "Sorry. It was an early morning."

"You'll want to stay awake. An old friend of yours is stopping by tonight."

"Who?" Micah asked.

She could tell them, but it served her brothers right to let their curiosity stew a bit longer. Smiling, she said, "Someone who inherited a farm on Zook Road."

The twins exchanged a disbelieving glance before Daniel asked, "Are you talking about Nate Zook?"

"He calls himself Nathaniel now."

"He's back in Paradise Springs?" he asked.

"Ja."

"It's been almost ten years since the last time we saw him." With a pensive expression, Micah rubbed his chin between his forefinger and thumb. "Remember, Daniel? He came out from Indiana to spend the summer with his grandparents the year after his family moved."

Daniel chuckled. "His *grossmammi* made us chocolate shoo-fly pie the day before he left. One of the best things I've ever tasted. Do you remember, Esther?"

"No." She was glad she had her back to them as she placed ham slices in the cast-iron fry pan. Her face was growing warm as she thought again of Nathaniel's visit and how she'd made a complete fool of herself. Hurrying to the cellar doorway, she got the bag of potatoes that had been harvested a few weeks ago. She'd make mashed potatoes tonight. Everyone liked them, and she could release some of her pent-up emotions while smashing them.

"Oh, that's right," Daniel said. "You decided you didn't want to play with us boys any longer. You thought it was a big secret why, but we knew."

She looked over her shoulder before she could halt herself. "You did?" How many more surprises was she going to have today? First, Nathaniel Zook showed up at her school, and now her brother was telling her he'd known why she stopped going to the Zook farm. Had Nathaniel told him about her brash stupidity of announcing she planned to marry him one day?

"Ja." Jabbing his brother with his elbow, Micah said, "You had a big crush on Nate. Giggled whenever you were around him."

She wanted to take them by the shoulders and shake them and tell them how wrong they were. She couldn't. That would be a lie. She'd had a big crush on Nathaniel. He was the only boy she knew who wasn't annoyed because she could outrun him or hit a ball as well as he did. He'd never tried to make her feel she was different from other girls because she preferred being outside to working beside her *mamm* in the house. Not once had he picked on her because she did well at school, like some of the other boys had.

That had happened long ago. She needed to put it out of her head. Nathaniel must have forgotten—or at least forgiven her—since he came to ask a favor today. She'd follow his lead for once and act as if the mortifying day had never happened.

"You don't know what you're talking about," Esther said, lifting her chin as she carried the potatoes to the sink to wash them. "I was a little girl."

"Who had a big crush on Nate Zook." Her brothers laughed as if Micah had said the funniest thing ever. "We'll have to watch and see if she drools when he walks in."

"Stop teasing your sister," *Mamm* said as she came through the door from the *dawdi haus*. She'd moved in preparation for Ezra's marriage. Though neither Ezra nor Leah spoke of their plans to marry, everyone suspected they'd be among the first couples having their intentions published at the next church Sunday.

"Well, she needs to marry someone," Micah said with a broad grin. "She can't seem to make up her mind about the guys around here. Just like Danny-boy can't decide on one girl." He poked his elbow at his twin again, but Daniel moved aside.

"Why settle for one when there are plenty of pretty ones willing to let me take them home?" Daniel asked.

Esther was startled to see his smile wasn't reflected

in his eyes. His jesting words were meant to hide his true feelings. The twins were popular with young people in their district and the neighboring ones. They were fun and funny. What was Daniel concealing behind his ready grin?

More questions, and she didn't need more questions. She already had enough without any answers. The marriage season for the Amish began in October. As it approached, she'd asked herself if she should try walking out with another young man. Maybe that would be the best way to put Alvin Lee and his betrayal out of her mind. But she wasn't ready to risk her heart again.

Better to be wise than to be sorry. How many times had she heard *Mamm* say those words? She'd discovered the wisdom in them by learning the truth the hard way. She'd promised herself to be extra careful with her heart from now on.

After giving her *mamm* a hug, Esther finished preparing their supper. She was grateful for *Mamm*'s assistance because she felt clumsy as she hadn't since she first began helping in the kitchen. Telling herself to focus, she avoided cutting herself as she peeled potatoes. Her brothers were too busy teasing each other to notice how her fingers shook.

Danki, Lord, for small blessings.

She put the reheated ham, buttered peas and a large bowl of mashed potatoes on the table. *Mamm* finished slicing the bread Esther had made before school that morning and put platters at either end along with butter and apple butter. While Esther retrieved the cabbage salad and chowchow from the refrigerator, her *mamm* filled a pitcher with water.

The door opened, and Ezra came in with a metal half-gallon milk can. In his other hand he carried a generous slab of his fragrant, homemade cheese. He called a greeting before stepping aside to let three more brothers enter. They'd been busy at the Stoltzfus Family Shops closer to the village of Paradise Springs. Amos set fresh apple cider from his grocery store in the center of the table.

As soon as they sat together at the table, Ezra, as the oldest son present, bowed his head. It was the signal for the meal's silent grace.

Esther quickly offered her thanks, then added a supplication that she'd be able to help Nathaniel without complications. To be honest, she'd enjoy teaching him how to raise alpacas and harvest the wondrously soft wool they grew.

As she raised her head when Ezra cleared his throat, she glanced around the table at her brothers and *mamm*. She had a *gut* life with her family and her scholars and her community. She didn't need adventure. Not her own or anyone else's. How she would have embarrassed her family if they'd heard of her partying with Alvin Lee and his friends! She could have lost her position as teacher, as well as shamed her family.

Learn from your failures, or you'll fail to learn. A poster saying that hung in the schoolroom. She needed to remember those words and hold them close to her heart. She vowed to do so, starting that very second.

As Nathaniel drove his buggy into the farm lane leading to the large white farmhouse where the Stoltzfus family lived, he couldn't keep from grinning. He'd looked forward to seeing them as much as he had his grandparents when he'd spent a summer in Paradise Springs years ago. Micah and Daniel had imaginations that had cooked up mischief to keep their summer days filled with adventures. Not even chores could slow down their laugh-filled hours.

Then there was Esther. She'd been brave enough to try anything and never quailed before a challenge. The twins had been less willing to accept every dare he posed. Not Esther. He remembered the buzz of excitement he'd felt the afternoon she'd agreed to jump from the second story hayloft if he did.

He knew he was going to have to be that gutsy if he hoped to save his grandparents' farm. It'd been in the family for generations, and he didn't want to be the one to sell it. Even if he couldn't have *kinder* of his own to inherit it, his two oldest sisters were already married with *bopplin*. One of them might want to take over the farm, and he didn't want to lose it because he hadn't learned quickly enough.

Esther agreeing to help him with the alpacas might be the saving grace he'd prayed for. If it wasn't, he could be defeated before he began.

No, I'm not going to think that way. I'm not going to give up before I've barely begun. He got out of the buggy. Things were going to get better. Starting now. He had to believe God's hands were upon the inheritance that gave him a chance to make his dream of running his own farm come true.

He strode toward the white house's kitchen door. Nobody used the front door except for church Sundays and funerals. The house and white outbuildings hadn't changed much in ten years. There was a third silo by the largest barn, and instead of the black-and-white cows Esther's *daed* used to milk, grayish-brown cattle stood in the pasture. The chicken coop was closer to the house than he remembered, and extra buggies and wagons were parked beneath the trees.

He paused at the door. He'd never knocked at the Stoltzfus house before, but somehow it didn't feel right to walk in. Too many years had passed since the last time he'd come to the farm.

"Why are you standing on the steps?" came a friendly female voice as the door swung open. "*Komm* in, Nate. We're about to enjoy some *snitz* pie."

Wanda Stoltzfus, Esther's *mamm*, looked smaller than he remembered. He knew she hadn't shrunk; he'd grown. Her hair had strands of gray woven through it, but her smile was as warm as ever.

"Did you make the pie?" he asked, delighted to see the welcome in eyes almost the same shade as her daughter's.

"Do you think I'd trust anyone, even my own *kinder*, with my super secret recipe for dried-apple pie while there's breath in these old bones?" She stepped aside and motioned for him to come in.

"You aren't old, Wanda," he replied.

"And you haven't lost an ounce of the charm you used as a boy to try to wheedle extra treats from me."

He heard a snicker and looked past her. Esther was at the stove, pouring freshly brewed *kaffi* into one cup after the other. The sound hadn't come from her, but his gaze had riveted on her. She looked pretty and somehow younger and more vulnerable now that she was barefoot and had traded her starched *kapp* for a dark kerchief over her golden hair. He could see the little girl she'd been transposed over the woman she had become, and his heart gave a peculiar little stutter.

What was that? He hadn't felt its like before, and he

wasn't sure what was causing it now. Esther was his childhood friend. Why was he nervous?

Hearing another laugh, Nathaniel pulled his gaze from her and looked at the table where six of the seven Stoltzfus brothers were gathered. Joshua, whom he'd recently heard had married again after the death of his first wife, and Ruth, the oldest, who had been wed long enough to have given her husband a houseful of *kinder*, were missing. A pulse of sorrow pinched at him because he noticed Ezra was sitting where Paul, the family's late patriarch, had sat. Paul had welcomed him into the family as if Nathaniel were one of his own sons.

Nathaniel stared at the men rising from the table. It was startling to see his onetime childhood playmates grown up. He'd known time hadn't stood still for them. Yet the change was greater than he'd guessed. Isaiah wore a beard that was patchy and sparse. He must be married, though Nathaniel hadn't heard about it. All the Stoltzfus brothers were tall, well-muscled from hard work and wore friendly smiles.

Then the twins opened their mouths and asked him how he liked running what they called the Paradise Springs Municipal Zoo. Nothing important had changed, he realized. They enjoyed teasing each other and everyone around them, and he was their chosen target tonight. Nothing they said was cruel. They poked fun as much at themselves as anyone else. Their eyes hadn't lost the mischievous glint that warned another prank was about to begin.

For the first time since he'd returned to Paradise Springs, he didn't feel like a stranger. He was among friends.

Nathaniel sat at the large table. When Esther put a

slice of pie and a steaming cup of *kaffi* in front of him, he thanked her. She murmured something before hurrying away to bring more cups to the table. He had no chance to talk to her because her brothers kept him busy with questions. He was amazed to learn that Jeremiah, who'd been all thumbs as a boy, now was a master woodworker, and Isaiah was a blacksmith as well as one of the district's ministers. Amos leaned over to whisper that Isaiah's young bride had died a few months earlier, soon after Isaiah had been chosen by lot to be the new minister.

Saddened by the family's loss, he knew he should wait until he had a chance to talk to Isaiah alone before he expressed his condolences. He sensed how hard Isaiah was trying to join in the *gut* humor around the table.

Nathaniel answered their questions about discovering the alpacas on the farm and explained how he planned to plant the fields in the spring. "Right now, the fields are rented to neighbors, so I can't cut a single blade of grass to feed those silly creatures this winter."

"You're staying in Paradise Springs?" Wanda asked.

"That's my plan." His parents weren't pleased he'd left Indiana, though they'd pulled up roots in Lancaster County ten years ago. He'd already received half a dozen letters from his *mamm* pleading for him to come home. She acted as if he'd left the Amish to join the *Englisch* world.

"*Wunderbaar*, Nate… I mean, Nathaniel." Wanda smiled.

"Call me whichever you wish. It doesn't matter."

"I know your family must be pleased to have you take over the farm that has been in Zook hands for generations. It is *gut* to know it'll continue in the family."

"Ja." He sounded as uncertain as he felt. The generations to come might be a huge problem. He reminded himself to be optimistic and focus on the here and now. Once he made the farm a success, his nephews and nieces would be eager to take it over.

His gaze locked with Esther's. He hadn't meant to let it happen, but he couldn't look away. There was much more to her now than the little girl she'd been. He had a difficult time imagining her at the teacher's desk instead of among the scholars, sending him and her brothers notes filled with plans for after school.

Esther the Pester was what they'd called her then, but he'd been eager to join in with the fun she proposed. He wondered if she were as avid to entertain her scholars. No wonder everyone praised her teaching.

Ezra said his name in a tone suggesting he'd been trying to get Nathaniel's attention. Breaking free of his memories was easier than cutting the link between his eyes and Esther's. He wasn't sure he could have managed it if she hadn't looked away.

Recalling what Ezra had asked, Nathaniel said, "I've got a lot to learn to be a proper farmer. Esther agreed to help me with the alpacas."

"Don't let her tell you Daniel and I tried roping hers," Micah said with a laugh. "It was an innocent misunderstanding."

"Misunderstanding? Yes," Esther retorted. "Innocent? I don't think so. Poor Pepe and Delfina were traumatized for weeks."

"The same amount of time it took to get the reek of their spit off me." Micah wrinkled his nose. "Watch out, Nathaniel. They're docile most of the time but they have a secret weapon. Their spit can leave you gagging for days."

Nathaniel grinned. "I'm glad you two learned that disgusting lesson instead of me." He noticed Esther was smiling broadly. "I hope, Ezra, you don't mind me asking you about a thousand questions about working the fields."

"Of course not, though it'd be better to wait to ask until after the first of the year." He reached for another piece of pie.

Nathaniel started to ask why, then saw the family's abruptly bland faces. Ezra must be getting married. His *mamm* and brothers and Esther were keeping the secret until the wedding was announced. They must like his future bride and looked forward to her becoming a part of their family along with any *kinder* she and Ezra might have.

He kept his sigh silent. Assuming he ever found a woman who would consider marrying him, having a single *kind* of his own might be impossible. He'd been thirteen when he was diagnosed with leukemia. That had been after the last summer he'd spent in Paradise Springs with his grandparents. For the next year, he'd undergone treatments and fought to recover. Chemo and radiation had defeated the cancer, but he'd been warned the chemo that had saved his life made it unlikely he'd ever be a *daed*. He thought he'd accepted it as God's will, but, seeing the quiet joy in Ezra Stoltzfus's eyes was a painful reminder of what he would never have. He couldn't imagine a woman agreeing to marry him once she knew the truth.

When the last of the pie was gone, the table cleared and thanks given once more, Nathaniel knew it was time to leave. Everyone had to be up before the sun in the morning.

As he stood, he asked as casually as he could, "Esther, will you walk to my buggy with me?"

Her brothers and *mamm* regarded him with as much astonishment as if he'd announced he wanted to discuss a trip to the moon. Did they think he was planning to court her? He couldn't, not when he couldn't give Esther *kinder*. She loved them. He'd seen that at the school.

"I've got a few questions about your scholars visiting the farm," he hurried to add.

"All right." Esther came to her feet with the grace she hadn't had as a little girl. Walking around the table, she went to the door. She pulled on her black sneakers and bent to tie them.

The night, when they stepped outside, was cool, but crisp in the way fall nights were. The stars seemed closer than during the summer, and the moon was beginning to rise over the horizon. It was a brilliant orange. Huge, it took up most of the eastern sky.

Under his boots, the grass was slippery with dew. It wouldn't be long before the dampness became frost. The seasons were gentler and slower here than in northern Indiana. He needed to become attuned to their pace again.

Esther's steps were soft as she walked beside him while they made arrangements for the scholars' trip. He smiled when she asked if it would be okay for the *kinder* to have their midday meal at the farm.

"That way, we can have time for desk work when we return," she said.

"I'll make sure I have drinks for the *kinder*, so they don't have to bring those."

"That's kind of you, Nathaniel." She offered him another warm smile. "I want to say *danki* again for helping me stop the fight this afternoon."

"Do you have many of them?"

"*Ja*, and Jacob seems to be involved in each one."

He frowned. "Is there something wrong with the boy that he can't settle disagreements other than with his fists?" The wrong question to ask, he realized when she bristled.

"Nothing is *wrong* with him." She took a steadying breath, then said more calmly, "Forgive me. You can't know how it is. Jacob has had a harder time than most kids. He lives with his *onkel*, actually his *daed*'s *onkel*. The man is too old to be taking care of a *kind*, but apparently he's the boy's sole relative. At least Jacob has him. The poor boy has seen things no *kind* should see."

"What do you mean?" He stopped beneath the great maple tree at the edge of the yard.

She explained how Jacob's parents had been killed and the boy badly hurt, physically and emotionally. Nathaniel's heart contracted with the thought of a *kind* suffering such grief.

"After the accident," she said, "we checked everywhere for other family, even putting a letter in *The Budget*."

He knew the newspaper aimed at and written by correspondents in plain communities was read throughout the world. "Nobody came forward?"

"Nobody." Her voice fell to a whisper. "Maybe that's why Jacob is angry. He believes everyone, including God, has abandoned him. He blames God for taking his *mamm* and *daed* right in front of his eyes. Why should he obey Jesus's request that we turn the other cheek and forgive those who treat us badly when, in Jacob's opinion, God has treated him worse than anyone on Earth could?"

"Anger at God eats at your soul. He has time to wait for your fury to run its course and still He forgives you."

"That sounds like the voice of experience."

"It is." He hesitated, wondering if he should tell her about the chemo. It was too personal a subject to share, even with Esther.

She said nothing, clearly expecting him to continue. When he didn't, she bid him good-night and started to turn away.

He put his hand on her arm as he'd done many times when they were kids. She looked at him, and the moonlight washed across her face. Who would have guessed a freckle-faced imp would mature into such a pretty woman? That odd sensation uncurled in his stomach again when she gazed at him, waiting for him to speak. Another change, because the Esther he'd known years ago wouldn't have waited on anything before she plunged headlong into her next adventure.

"*Danki* for agreeing to teach me about alpacas."

He watched her smile return and brighten her face. "I know how busy you are, but without your help I might have to sell the flock."

"Herd," she said with a laugh. "Sheep are a flock. Alpacas are a herd."

"See? I'm learning already."

"You've got much more to learn."

He grinned. "You used to like when I had to listen to you."

"Still do. I'll let you know when I've contacted the scholars' parents, and we'll arrange a day for them to visit." She patted his arm and ran into the house, her skirts fluttering behind her.

With a chuckle, he climbed into his buggy. He might not know a lot about alpacas, but he knew the lessons to come wouldn't be boring as long as Esther was involved.

Chapter Three

Nathaniel stepped down from his wagon and past the pair of mules hooked to it. There would be about twenty-two *kinder* along with, he guessed, at least one or two *mamms* to help oversee the scholars. Add in Esther and her assistant teacher. It was a small load, so it would give the mules, Sal and Gal, some gentle exercise. Tomorrow, he needed them to fetch a large load of hay. He'd store it in the barn to feed the animals during the winter.

The scholars were milling about in front of the school, their excited voices like a flock of blue jays. He was glad he'd left his *mutze* coat, the black wool coat plain men wore to church services, home on the warm morning and had his black vest on over his white shirt. His black felt hat was too hot, and he'd trade it for his straw one as soon as he got to the farm.

A boy ran over to be the first on the wagon. He halted, and Nathaniel recognized him from the scab on the corner of his mouth. It was the legacy of the punch Benny had taken from Jacob Fisher last week.

"Gute mariye," Nathaniel said with a smile.

The boy watched him with suspicion, saying nothing.

"How's the lip?" Nathaniel asked. "It looks sore."

"It is," Benny replied grudgingly.

"Have your *mamm* put a dab of hand lotion on it to keep the skin soft, so it can heal. Try to limit your talking. You don't want to keep breaking it open."

The boy started to answer, then raised his eyebrows in a question.

"A day or two will allow it to heal. If you've got to say something, think it over first and make sure it's worth the pain that follows."

Benny nodded, then his eyes widened when he understood the true message in Nathaniel's suggestion. Keeping his mouth closed would help prevent him from saying something that could lead to a fight. The boy looked at the ground, then claimed his spot at the very back of the wagon bed where the ride would be the bumpiest.

Hoping what he said would help Esther by preventing another fight, Nathaniel walked toward the school. He was almost there when she stepped out and closed the door behind her. Today she wore a dark blue dress beneath her black apron. The color was the perfect foil for her eyes and her hair, which was the color of spun caramel.

"Right on time, Nathaniel," she said as she came down the steps. He tried to connect the prim woman she was now with the enthusiastic *kind* she'd been. It was almost impossible, and he couldn't help wondering what had quashed her once high spirits.

"I know you don't like to wait," he said instead of asking the questions he wanted to.

"Neither does anyone else." She put her arms around

two of the *kinder* closest to her, and they looked at her with wide grins.

He helped her get the smaller ones on the wagon where they'd be watched by the older scholars. He wasn't surprised when Jacob found a place close to the front. The boy sat as stiffly as a cornstalk, making it clear he didn't want anyone near him.

Esther glanced at Nathaniel. He could tell she was frustrated at not being able to reach the *kind*. He'd added Jacob to his prayers and hoped God would bring the boy comfort. As He'd helped Nathaniel during the horrific rounds of chemo and the wait afterward to discover if the cancer had been vanquished.

"I'll keep an eye on him," he whispered.

"Me, too." She smiled again, but it wasn't as bright. After she made sure nobody had forgotten his or her lunch box, she sat on the seat with him.

He'd hoped to get time to chat with Esther during the fifteen minute drive to his farm, but she spent most of the ride looking over her shoulder to remind the scholars not to move close to the edges or to suggest a song for them to sing. Her assistant and the two *mamms* who'd joined them were kept busy with making sure the lunch boxes didn't bounce off. As they passed farmhouses, neighbors waved to them, and the *kinder* shouted they were going to see the alpacas.

"Nobody has any secrets with them around, do they?" Nathaniel grinned as the scholars began singing again.

"None whatsoever." Esther laughed. "It's one of the first lessons I learned. I love my job so I don't mind having everything I do and say at school repeated to parents each night."

"It sounds, from what I've heard, as if the parents are pleased."

A flush climbed her cheeks. "The *kinder* are important to all of us."

He looked past the mules' ears so she couldn't see his smile. Esther was embarrassed by his compliment. If the scholars hadn't been in earshot, he would have teased her about blushing.

Telling the *kinder* to hold on tight, he turned the wagon in at the lane leading to his grandparents' farm. To *his* farm. This morning, he'd received another letter from his *mamm*, begging him to return to Indiana instead of following his dreams in Paradise Springs. He must find a gentle way to let her know, once and for all, that he wanted to remain in Lancaster County. And he'd suggest she find the best words to let Vernita Miller know, as well. He didn't intend to marry Vernita, no matter how often the young woman had hinted he should. She'd find someone else. Perhaps his *gut* friend Dwayne Kempf who was sweet on her.

He shook thoughts of his *mamm*, Indiana and Vernita out of his head as he drew in the reins and stopped the wagon near the barn. Like the house, it needed a new coat of white paint. He'd started on the big project of fixing all the buildings when he could steal time from taking care of the animals, but, so far, only half of one side of the house was done.

"There they are!" came a shout from the back.

Jumping down, Nathaniel smiled when he saw the excited *kinder* pointing at the alpacas near the pasture fence. He heard a girl describe them as "adorable." Their long legs and neck were tufted with wool. Around their faces, more wool puffed like an aura.

The alpacas raced away when the scholars poured off the wagon.

"Where are they going?" a little girl asked him as he lifted her down.

"To get the others," he replied, though he knew the skittish creatures wanted to flee as far as possible from the noisy *kinder*.

Esther put her finger to her lips. "You must be quiet. Be like little mice sneaking around a sleeping cat."

The youngest scholars giggled. She asked each little one to take the hand of an older child. A few of the boys, including Jacob, which was no surprise, refused to hold anyone else's hand. Esther told them to remain close to the others and not to speak loudly.

"Where do you want us, Nathaniel?" she asked. "By the fence is probably best. What do you think?"

"You're the expert."

She led the *kinder* to the wooden fence backed by chicken wire, making sure the littler ones could see. "Can you name some of the alpacas' cousins?"

"Llamas!" called a boy.

She nodded, but motioned for him to lower his voice as the alpacas shifted nervously. "Llamas are one of their cousins. Can you tell me another?"

"Horses?" asked a girl.

"No."

"Cows?"

"No." She pointed at the herd after letting the scholars make a few more guesses. "Alpacas are actually cousins of camels."

"Like the ones the Wise Men rode?" asked Jacob.

Nathaniel saw Esther's amazement, though it was quickly masked. She was shocked the boy was participating, but he heard no sign of it in her voice when she assured Jacob he was right. That set off a buzz of more questions from the scholars.

The boy turned to look at the pasture, again separating himself from the others though he stood among them. The single breakthrough was a small victory. He could tell by the lilt in Esther's voice how delighted she'd been with Jacob's question.

The scholars' eager whispers followed Nathaniel as he entered the pasture through the barn. He'd try to herd the alpacas closer so the *kinder* could get a better look at them. His hopes were dashed when the alpacas evaded him as they always did. They resisted any attempt to move them closer to the scholars. If he jogged to the right, they went left. If he moved forward, they trotted away and edged around him. He could almost hear alpaca laughter.

"Let me," Esther called. She bunched up her dress and climbed over the fence as if she were one of the *kinder.* She brought a pair of thin branches, each about a yard long. As she crossed the pasture, she motioned for him to stand by the barn.

"Watch the *kinder,*" she said. "I'll get an alpaca haltered, so we can bring it closer for them to see."

Curious about how she was going to do that, he watched her walk toward the herd with slow, even steps. She spoke softly, nonsense words from what he could discern.

She held the branches out to either side of her. He realized she was using them like a shepherd's crook to move the alpacas into the small shed at the rear of the pasture. He edged forward to see what she'd do once they were inside. He'd wondered what the shed with its single

large pen was for. He hadn't guessed it was to corner the
alpacas to make it easier to handle them.

She lifted a halter off a peg once the alpacas were
in the pen. She chose a white-and-brown one who was
almost as tall as she was. Moving to the animal's left,
she gently slid the halter over its nose and behind its
ears. The animal stood as docile as a well-trained dog,
nodding its head when Esther checked to make sure
the buckled halter was high enough on the nose that it
wouldn't prevent the animal from breathing.

Latching a rope to the halter, Esther walked the alpaca from the shed. The other animals trotted behind
her, watching her. Esther stayed on the alpaca's left side
and an arm's length away. The alpaca followed her easily,
but shied as she neared the fence where the *kinder* stood.

One *kind* pushed closer to the fence. Jacob! The boy's
gaze was riveted on the alpaca. His usual anger was fading into something that wasn't a smile, but close.

Nathaniel wondered if Esther had noticed, but
couldn't tell because her back was to him. Again she
warned the scholars to be silent. Their eyes were curious but none of them stuck their fingers past the fence.

Esther looked over her shoulder at him. "You can
come closer. Stay to her left side."

"You made it look easy," Nathaniel replied with admiration.

"Any task is easy when you know what you're doing."
She winked at the scholars. "Like multiplication tables,
ain't so?"

The younger ones giggled.

"Be careful it doesn't spit at you," Nathaniel warned
the *kinder*.

"It won't." Esther patted the alpaca's head as the scholars edged back.

"Don't be sure. When I put them out this morning, this one started spitting at the others. She hasn't acted like that before."

"Were the males in there, too?"

He nodded. Before he'd gone to the school, he'd spent a long hour separating the males out because he feared they'd be aggressive near the *kinder*.

"Then," Esther said with a smile, "my guess is she's going to have a cria."

"A what?"

She laughed and nudged his shoulder with hers. "A *boppli*, Nathaniel."

The ordinary motion had anything but an ordinary effect on his insides. A ripple of awareness rushed through him like a powerful train. Had she felt it, too? He couldn't be sure because the scholars clapped their hands in delight. She was suddenly busy keeping the alpaca from pulling away in fear at the noise, but she calmed the animal.

"I'm going to need you to tell me what to do," Nathaniel said, glad his voice sounded calmer than he felt as he struggled to regain his equilibrium.

"There's no hurry. An alpaca is pregnant for at least eleven months, but she'll need to be examined by the vet to try to determine how far along she is."

As she continued to talk about the alpacas to her scholars, he sent a grateful prayer to God for Esther's help. His chances of making the farm a success were much greater than they'd been. He wasn't going to waste a bit of the time or the information she shared with him.

No, he assured himself as he watched her. He wasn't going to waste a single second.

Esther walked to the farmhouse, enjoying the sunshine. The trees along the farm lane were aflame with color against the bright blue sky. Not a single cloud blemished it. Closer to the ground, mums in shades of gold, orange and dark red along the house's foundation bobbed on a breeze that barely teased her nape.

She'd left the scholars with Nathaniel while she checked the alpacas. Though he didn't know much about them, he'd made sure they were eating well. She'd seen no sores on their legs. They hadn't been trying to get out of the pasture, so they must be content with what he provided.

Hearing shouts from the far side of the house, she walked in that direction. She hadn't planned to take so long with the alpacas, but it'd been fun to be with the silly creatures again. Their fleece was exceptionally soft, and their winter coats were growing in well. By the time they were sheared in the spring, Nathaniel would have plenty of wool to sell.

She came around the house and halted. On the sloping yard, Nathaniel was surrounded by the scholars. Jay, the oldest, was helping keep the *kinder* in a line. What were they doing?

Curious, she walked closer. She was amazed to see cardboard boxes torn apart and placed end to end on the grass. Two boxes were intact. As she watched, Nathaniel picked up a little girl and set her in one box. She giggled and gripped the front of it.

"All set?" he asked.

"Ja!" the *kind* shouted.

Nathaniel glanced at Jay and gave the box a slight shove. It sailed down the cardboard "slide" like a toboggan on snow. He kept pace with it on one side while Jay did on the other. They caught the box at the end of the slide before it could tip over and spill the *kind* out.

Picking her up again, Nathaniel swung her around. Giggling, she ran up the hill as a bigger boy jumped into the other box. His legs hung out the front, but he pushed with his hands to send himself down the slide. Nathaniel swung the other box out of the way just in time.

Everyone laughed and motioned for the boxes to be brought back for the next ride. As the older boy climbed out, Esther saw it was Benny. He beamed as he gathered the boxes to carry them to the top. Nathaniel clapped him on the shoulder and grinned.

She went to stand by the porch where she could watch the *kinder* play. She couldn't take her eyes off Nathaniel. He looked as happy as he had when they were *kinder* themselves. He clearly loved being with the youngsters. He'd be a *wunderbaar daed*. Seeing him with her scholars, she could imagine him acting like her own *daed*.

Her most precious memories of *Daed* were when he'd come into the house at midday and pick her up. They'd bounce around the kitchen table singing a silly song until *Mamm* pretended to be irritated about how they were in the way. Then they'd laugh together, and *Daed* would set her in her chair before chasing her brothers around the living room. If he caught them, he'd tickle them until they squealed or *Mamm* called everyone to the table. As they bent their heads in silent grace, their shared joy had been like a glow around them.

Watching Nathaniel with the *kinder*, she wanted

that for him. Too bad she and he were just friends. Otherwise—

Where had *that* thought come from? He was her buddy, her partner in crime, her competitor to see who could run the fastest or climb the highest. She *had* told him she'd marry him when they were little kids, something that made her blush when she thought of how outrageously she'd acted, but they weren't *kinder* any longer.

When Nathaniel called a halt to the game, saying it was time for lunch, the youngsters tried not to show their disappointment. They cheered when he said he had fresh cider waiting for them on a picnic table by the kitchen door.

They raced past Esther to get their lunch boxes. She smiled as she went to help Nathaniel collect the pieces of cardboard.

"Quite a game you have here," she said. "Did you make it up?"

As he folded the long cardboard strips and set them upright in one of the boxes, he shook his head. "Not me alone. It's one we played in Indiana. We invented it the summer after I couldn't go sledding all winter."

"Why? Were you sick?"

"Ja."

"All winter?"

"You know how *mamms* can be. Always worrying." He gathered the last bits of cardboard and dropped them into the other box. Brushing dirt off himself, he grimaced as he tapped his left knee. "Grass stains on my *gut* church clothes. *Mamm* wouldn't be happy to see that."

He looked very handsome in his black vest and trousers, which gave his dark hair a ruddy sheen. The white shirt emphasized his strong arms and shoulders. She'd noticed his shoulders when she tumbled against him at school.

"If you want," she said when she realized she was staring. "I'll clean them."

"I can't ask you to do that." He carried the boxes to the porch. "You've got enough to do keeping up with your brothers."

"One more pair of trousers won't make any difference." She smiled as she walked with him toward the kitchen door. "Trust me."

"I do, and my alpacas do, too. It was amazing how you calmed them."

"I'll teach you."

"I don't know if I can convince them to trust me as they do you. It might be impossible. Though obviously not for Esther Stoltzfus, the alpaca whisperer."

She laughed, then halted when she saw a buggy driving at top speed along the farm lane. Even from a distance, she recognized her brother Isaiah driving it. She glanced at Nathaniel, then ran to where the buggy was stopping. Only something extremely important would cause Isaiah to leave his blacksmith shop in the middle of the day.

He climbed out, his face lined with dismay. "Esther, where are the *kinder*?"

"Behind the house having lunch."

"Gut." He looked from her to Nathaniel. "There's no way to soften this news. Titus Fisher has had a massive stroke and is on his way to the hospital."

Esther gasped and pressed her hands to her mouth.

"Are you here to get the boy?" asked Nathaniel.

"I'm not sure he should go to the hospital until Titus

is stable." Isaiah turned to her. "What do you think, Esther?"

"I think he needs to be told his *onkel* is sick, but nothing more now. No need to scare him. Taking him to the hospital can wait until we know more."

"That's what I thought, but you know him better than I do." He sighed. "The poor *kind*. He's already suffered enough. Tonight—"

"He can stay here," Nathaniel said quietly.

"Are you sure?" her brother asked, surprised.

"I've got plenty of room," Nathaniel said, "and the boy seems fascinated by my alpacas."

Isaiah looked at her for confirmation.

She nodded, knowing it was the best solution under the circumstances.

"I'll let Reuben know." He sighed again. "Just in case."

"Tell the bishop that Jacob can stay here as long as he needs to," Nathaniel said.

"That should work out…unless his *onkel* dies. Then the Bureau of Children and Family Services will have to get involved."

Nathaniel frowned, standing as resolute as one of the martyrs of old.

Before he could retort, Esther said, "Let's deal with one problem at a time." She prayed it wouldn't get to that point. And if it did, there must be some plan to give Jacob the family he needed without *Englisch* interference. She had no idea what, but they needed to figure it out fast.

Chapter Four

Esther looked around for Jacob as soon as her brother left. Isaiah was bound for their bishop's house. He and Reuben planned to hire an *Englisch* driver to take them to the hospital where they would check on Titus Fisher.

She wasn't surprised Jacob had left the other scholars and gone to watch the alpacas. The boy stood by the fence, his fingers stuck through the chicken wire in an offer for the shy beasts to come over and sniff them. The alpacas were ignoring him from the far end of the pasture.

The sight almost broke her heart. Jacob, who was small for his age and outwardly fragile, stood alone as he reached out to connect with another creature.

"Are you okay?" asked Nathaniel as he walked beside her toward the pasture.

"Not really." She squared her shoulders, knowing she must not show the *kind* how sorry she felt for him. Jacob reacted as badly to pity as he did to teasing. He'd endured too much during his short life.

Suddenly she stopped and put out her arm to halt Nathaniel. He frowned at her, but, putting her fingers to her lips, she whispered, "Shhh…"

In the pasture, one of the younger alpacas inched away from the others, clearly curious about the boy who had been standing by the fence for so long. The light brown female stretched out her neck and sniffed the air as if trying to determine what sort of animal Jacob was. Glancing at the rest of the herd, she took one step, then another toward him.

The boy didn't move, but Esther guessed his heart was trying to beat its way out of his chest. A smile tipped his lips, the first one she'd ever seen on his face.

In the distance, the voices of the other scholars fluttered on the air, but Nathaniel and Esther remained as silent as Jacob. The alpaca's curiosity overcame her shyness, and she continued toward the boy. His smile broadened on every step, but he kept his outstretched fingers steady.

The alpaca paused an arm's length away, then took another step. She extended her head toward his fingertips, sniffing and curious.

Beside her, Esther heard Nathaniel whisper, "Keep going, girl. He needs you now."

Her heart was touched by his empathy for the *kind*. Nathaniel's generous spirit hadn't changed. He'd always been someone she could depend on, the very definition of a *gut* friend. He still was, offering kindness to a lonely boy. Her fingers reached out to his arm, wanting to squeeze it gently to let him know how much she appreciated his understanding of what Jacob needed.

Her fingers halted midway between them as a squeal came from near the house where the other scholars must be playing a game. At the sound, the alpaca whirled and loped back to the rest of the herd.

"Almost," Jacob muttered under his breath.

Walking to the boy, Esther fought her instinct to put her hand on his shoulder. That would send him skittering away like the curious alpaca. "It'll take them time to trust you, Jacob, but you've made a *gut* beginning."

When he glanced at her, for once his face wasn't taut with determination to hide his pain. She saw something she'd never seen there before.

Hope.

"Do you think so?" he asked.

She nodded. She must be as cautious with him as she was with the alpacas. "It'll take time and patience on your part, but eventually they learn to trust."

"Eventually?" His face hardened into an expression no *kind* should ever wear. "I guess that's that, then. We'll be leaving for school soon, ain't so?"

He'd given her the opening to tell him the bad news Isaiah had brought. She must tell him the truth now, but she must be careful how she told him until they were sure about Titus Fisher's prognosis.

"Jacob, I need to tell you about something that's happened," she began.

"If Jay said it was my fault, he's lying!" Jacob clenched his hands at his sides. "Benny tipped over Jay's glass, but said I did it. I didn't! I always tell the truth!"

Tears welled in the boy's eyes, and she saw his desperate need for her to believe him. And she did. Unlike some *kinder*, Jacob always admitted what he'd done wrong…if he were caught.

She squatted in front of him, so her eyes were even with his. Aware of Nathaniel behind her, she said quietly, "Nobody has said anything about a glass. This has nothing to do with the other *kinder*."

"Then what?" He was growing more wary by the second.

"I wanted to let you know your *onkel* isn't feeling well, so he went to see some *doktors* who will try to help him."

"Is it his heart?" Jacob's hands loosened, and he folded his arms over his narrow chest. Was he trying to protect himself?

When she glanced at Nathaniel, he looked as shocked as she felt at the forthright question. Clearly the boy was aware of his *onkel*'s deteriorating health. Jacob Fisher was a smart *kind*. She mustn't forget that, as the other scholars did far too often, underestimating his intelligence as well as how brittle his patience was.

"Ja," she answered. "The *doktors* want to observe him. That means—"

"They want to watch what his heart does so they can find out why it's giving him trouble." He gave a careless shrug, but he couldn't hide the fear burning in his eyes. *"Onkel* Titus explained to me the last time he went to the clinic."

She wanted to let him know it was okay to show his distress, but she wouldn't push. *Ja*, he was scared, but Titus had prepared the boy. She reminded herself that Jacob didn't know the full extent of what had happened. For now, it would be better not to frighten him further. She didn't want to think of what would happen if his *onkel* didn't recover. If she did, she wouldn't be able to hold back the tears prickling her eyes.

And that would scare Jacob more.

* * *

Nathaniel saw Esther struggling to hold on to her composure. He should have urged her to let him talk to Jacob alone. Unlike him, she knew Titus Fisher, and she must be distressed by the old man's stroke.

He drew her to her feet. He tried to ignore the soft buzz where his palms were spread across her arms. Releasing her because he needed to focus on the boy, he was amazed when the sensation still coursed along his hands.

Trying to ignore it, he said, "Jacob, under the circumstances, I think Esther would agree with me when I say you don't need to go back to school today."

"I don't?" Glee brightened his face for a moment, then it vanished. "Then I'll have to go to my *onkel*'s house by myself."

Nathaniel tried not to imagine what the boy was thinking. The idea of returning to an empty house where he'd be more alone than ever must be horrifying to Jacob. Knowing he must pick his words with care, he said, "I thought you might want to stay here."

"With the alpacas?" Jacob's eyes filled with anticipation.

Nathaniel struggled to keep his smile in place as he wondered if that expression would have been visible on Jacob's face more often if he hadn't watched his parents die and been sent to live with an elderly *onkel*. Titus Fisher had provided him with a *gut* home, or as *gut* as he could. The old man had protected his great-nephew from the realities of his failing health by telling him enough to make this moment easier for the boy.

What would Jacob—or Esther—say if he revealed how his own childhood had been filled with *doktors* and fear? His *mamm* had overreacted any time he got a cold, and his *daed* had withdrawn. If it hadn't been for their *Englisch* neighbor, Reggie O'Donnell, who'd welcomed Nathaniel at his greenhouses whenever he needed an escape, there would have been no break from the drama at home. The retired engineer had let Nathaniel assist and never made him talk or wash his hands endlessly or avoid playing with other *kinder* because he might get some germ that would bring on another bout of what they called "the scourge."

Though the *Englisch doktors* had assured his parents that, upon the completion of the treatments, Nathaniel had no more chance than any other person of contracting cancer again, they never could let go of their fear. He suspected that was one of the reasons his *mamm* insisted he return to Indiana. She wanted to keep an eye on him every second to make sure the scourge didn't return.

Was Titus Fisher a sanctuary for Jacob as Reggie had been for Nathaniel? Someone who didn't talk about the past or what might await in the future? Had he, like Reggie, been someone with a heart big enough to offer a haven for a lonely, lost *kind*?

Grief for the old man and the boy hammered Nathaniel. "*Ja*," he said, "you can stay here with me and the alpacas, if you'd like."

"And if I don't like?" Jacob asked cautiously.

Esther looked away, and he knew she was having difficulty keeping her feelings from showing. As he was. No *kind* Jacob's age should have to ask such a question. The boy had learned life could change in the blink of an eye. He probably hadn't had any say in where he would go after his parents' funeral.

"Then other arrangements will be made for you, and you can come and visit the alpacas."

Jacob shook his head. "No, I want to stay here. I think I can get one of them to come to me if I've got enough time."

"Then it's settled." Nathaniel tried to curb the sudden disquiet rising in him at the thought of being responsible for the boy. *Dear Lord, help me know the right things to do and say while he's here.* He forced a smile. "We'll work together to convince the alpacas to trust us. It'll be fun."

"It will!" The boy turned to look at the herd again. "Let's start now."

"I have to take everyone back to school."

The boy's shoulders slumped. "Can I stay here? *Onkel* Titus let me stay by myself."

Unsure if Jacob was being truthful or not, in spite of his assertion that he always was honest, Nathaniel hesitated.

Esther didn't. "If it's okay with you, Nathaniel, I can drive everyone to school. I'll take your wagon to our farm tonight. You can come and get it when it's convenient."

Again he hesitated. He'd planned to leave early tomorrow to get the hay for winter feedings, but those plans must change.

"All right," he said. "I'll help you hook Sal and Gal to the wagon. Do you know how to handle mules?"

"*Ja.* A little, but my brothers will know because *Daed* had a team to plow the fields. Ezra will make sure they're taken care of tonight."

He had no choice but to agree or upset Jacob further.

He couldn't blame the boy for not wanting to spend more time with his classmates, especially now.

"I'll be right back," Nathaniel said.

"Can I go into the pasture?" asked Jacob.

"Maybe later tonight when I feed them. Let's see how they're behaving then."

He thought the boy would argue, but Jacob nodded. "I'll wait here for you."

For a moment, Nathaniel wished the boy had protested like a regular kid. He remembered times, especially when he was going through chemo, when he'd found himself trying to be *gut* so he didn't upset the adults around him more. It hadn't been easy to swallow his honest reactions. His respect for Jacob grew, but the boy's maturity also concerned him. A *kind* needed to be a *kind*, not some sort of miniature adult.

When he said as much to Esther as they walked into the barn to get the mules, she sighed and stole a glance at where the boy was gazing at the alpacas once more. "I worry about him when he's cooperative and when he's fighting. It's as if he can't find a middle path."

"He probably can't. When everything inside you is in a turmoil, it's hard to trust your own feelings. Most especially when you've let them loose in the past and people haven't reacted well. Instead they've told you how you should feel so many times you begin to wonder if they're right and you're wrong."

She paused as he kept walking toward where he kept the harnesses for the mules. When he turned to see why she'd stopped, she said, "I hadn't thought about it like that."

Emotions he couldn't decipher scuttled across her face. He wanted to ask what she was thinking, but satisfying his curiosity would have to wait. She hurried past him, murmuring how she'd told the scholars' *mamms* she'd have everyone back by now. They'd spent more than an hour longer at the farm than she'd planned.

As he put Sal and Gal into place and hooked them to the wagon, Nathaniel glanced at Jacob standing by the alpacas' pasture, and then to the other *kinder* racing about by the house. The difference was unsettling, and he wondered if it was possible for Jacob to become carefree again. He had to believe so.

He looked across the mules at Esther, who was checking the reins. "Do you think we should let him continue to believe his *onkel*'s heart is why Titus was taken to the hospital?"

"I don't know." Her expression matched her unsteady words. "Let me talk to Isaiah when he gets back."

"A *gut* idea."

"Are you sure you want Jacob to stay with you? Is that why you asked?"

"No. I'm sure staying here is best for him now. The boy needs something to do to get his mind off the situation, and the alpacas can help."

She nodded. When she called to the other *kinder* to pack their things and prepare to leave, there were the protests Nathaniel had expected to hear. She handled each one with humor and serenity. She was a stark contrast to his *mamm* and his older sisters who saw everything as a potential tragedy.

He smiled as the scholars clambered onto the flatbed. When they passed him, each of them said, *"Danki."* Telling them to have a *gut* ride to school, he held his hand out to assist Esther onto the seat.

She regarded him with surprise, and he had to fight

not to smile. Now *that* reaction reminded him of Esther the Pester, who'd always asserted she could do anything the older boys did…and all by herself.

Despite that, she accepted his help. The scent of her shampoo lingered in his senses. He was tempted to hold on to her soft fingers, but he released them as soon as she was sitting. He was too aware of the *kinder* and other women gathered behind her.

She picked up the reins and leaned toward him. "If it becomes too difficult for you, bring him to our house."

"We'll be fine." At that moment, he meant it. When her bright blue eyes were close to his, he couldn't imagine being anything but fine.

Then she looked away, and the moment was over. She slapped the reins and drove the wagon toward the road. He watched it go. A sudden shiver ran along him. The breeze was damp and chilly, something he hadn't noticed while gazing into Esther's pretty eyes.

The sound of the rattling wagon vanished in the distance, and he turned to see Jacob standing by the fence, his fingers through the chicken wire again in the hope an alpaca would come to him. The *kind* had no idea of what could lie ahead for him.

Take him into Your hands, Lord. He's going to need Your comfort in the days to come. Make him strong to face what the future brings, but let him be weak enough to accept help from us.

Taking a deep breath, Nathaniel walked toward the boy. He'd agreed to take care of Jacob and offer him a haven at the farm. Now he had to prove he could.

Chapter Five

As Jacob helped with the afternoon chores, which included cleaning up after the alpacas and refilling their water troughs, Nathaniel watched closely. He knew Esther would want to know how the boy did in the wake of the news about his *onkel*. She worried about him as if he were her own *kind*. Nathaniel suspected she was that way with each of her scholars.

Jacob didn't say much, but he was comfortable doing hard work. Nathaniel wondered how many of the chores at Titus Fisher's house had become Jacob's responsibility as the old man's health declined. He seemed happy to remain behind, which was no surprise. A chance to skip school was something any kid would enjoy, but Nathaniel couldn't help wondering what the boy was thinking.

One thing he knew from his own childhood. Growing boys were always hungry.

Flashing Jacob a smile and a wink, he asked, "How about grabbing a snack before we feed the alpacas?"

"Whatcha got?"

Nathaniel chuckled as he motioned for the boy to follow him toward the house. Jacob seemed to walk a fine line between being a *kind* and being a wraith who floated through each day, not connecting with anyone else.

"I know there's church spread in the fridge," he answered.

Jacob grinned, and Nathaniel was glad he'd guessed what the boy would like. There weren't too many people who didn't enjoy the combination of peanut butter and marshmallow creme. Keeping it around allowed him to slap together a quick sandwich when he had scant time for dinner or was too tired to cook anything for supper.

"What else do you have to eat with it?" Jacob asked.

"We'll look through the kitchen. A treasure hunt without a map. Who knows what we might find?"

"As long as it's not growing green stuff." Excitement blossomed in Jacob's eyes.

Nathaniel laughed and ruffled the boy's hair. Jacob stiffened for a second, then relaxed with a smile.

The poor kid! Did anyone treat him as a *kind* or did others think of him solely as his sad experiences? The boy needed a chance to be a boy. Nathaniel knew that with every inch of his being. After having his own parents, with their *gut* intentions, nearly deny him his own chance to be a kid, he didn't want to see the same happen to another *kind*.

He wasn't going to let that occur. God had brought Jacob into his life for a reason, and it might be as simple as Nathaniel being able to offer him an escape, temporary though it might be, into a normal childhood. Reggie had given that to him. Now Nathaniel could do the same for Jacob.

With a laugh, he said, "You've got to be tired after tidying up."

"A bit."

"*Gut*. Then you won't be able to beat me to the kitchen door." With no more warning, Nathaniel loped away.

A moment passed, and he wondered if his attempt to get Jacob to play had failed. Then, with a whoop, the boy sped past him. Nathaniel lengthened his stride, but the *kind* reached the door before he could. Whirling to face him, Jacob pumped his arms in a victory dance.

Nathaniel let him cheer for a few moments and didn't remind him it wasn't the Amish way to celebrate beating someone else. There was time enough for those lessons later. For now, Jacob needed to feel like a kid.

"Well done." He clapped the boy on the shoulder. "Next time, I'll beat you."

"Don't be so sure." As Jacob smiled, his brown eyes were filled with humor instead of his usual lost expression.

Nathaniel laughed, thinking how pleased Esther would be when he shared this moment with her tomorrow. He opened the door and ushered the boy into a kitchen that looked the same as it had the day he'd arrived from Indiana for his summer visit so many years ago. The kitchen was a large room, but filled to capacity with furniture, as the living room was. There were enough chairs of all shapes and sizes to host a Sunday church service. His grandparents had been fond of auctions, but he'd been astounded when he arrived to discover the house chock-full of furnishings.

Nathaniel had stored many chairs and two dressers from the living room in an outbuilding, which was now full. He had to find other places to put the rest until there was a charity auction to which he could donate them. Until then he had to wend his way through an obstacle course of chairs every morning and night to reach the stairs.

Jacob walked in and sniffed. "This place smells like *Onkel* Titus's house."

"In what way?" He hoped something familiar would make the boy feel more at home.

"Full of old stuff and dust." He looked at Nathaniel. "Don't grown-ups ever throw anything out?"

He grinned. "Not my grandparents. My *grossmammi* saved the tabs from plastic bags. She always said, 'Use it up, wear it out—'"

"'…make it do or do without,'" finished Jacob with an abrupt grin. "*Onkel* Titus says the same thing. A lot." He glanced around. "Don't you think they could get by with a lot less stuff?"

"I know I could. If you can find an empty chair, bring it to the table while I make some sandwiches."

That brought a snort of something that might have been rusty laughter from the boy, but could have been disgust with the state of the house. Nathaniel didn't look at Jacob to determine which. Getting the boy to smile was *wunderbaar*. As they had an impromptu supper, with Nathaniel eating two sandwiches and Jacob three, he let the boy take the lead in deciding the topics of conversation.

There was only one. The alpacas. Jacob had more questions than Nathaniel could answer. Time after time, he had to reply that Jacob needed to ask Esther. The boy would nod, then ask another question. That continued while they got the alpacas ready for the night.

Nathaniel hid his smile when he heard Jacob chatter like a regular kid. He thanked God for putting a love for alpacas in his *grossmammi*'s heart, so the creatures could touch a lonely boy's. God's methods were splendid, and Nathaniel sent up a grateful prayer as he walked with Jacob back to the house when their chores were done.

Leading the boy upstairs—where there were yet more chairs—he smiled when Jacob yawned broadly. He opened a door across the hall from his own bedroom. It was a room he'd had some success in clearing out. In the closet were stairs leading to the attic, where he'd hoped there might be room to store furniture. However, like the rest of the house, it was already full.

"Here's where you'll sleep." Nathaniel was glad he'd kept the bed made so the room looked welcoming. He'd slept on the bed with its black and white and blue quilt the time he came to stay with his grandparents. Pegs on the wall waited for clothes, and a small table held the storybooks Nathaniel had read years ago. The single window gave a view of the pasture beyond the main barn.

"I can see them!" crowed Jacob, rushing around the iron bed to peer out the window. "The alpacas! They're right out there."

"They'll be there until I move them to another pasture in a couple of weeks."

The boy whirled. "Why do you have to move them?" His tone suggested Nathaniel was doing that to be cruel to him and the animals.

"If I don't move them, they'll be hungry." He tried to keep his voice calm. The boy needed to learn that not everything was an attack on him, but how did you teach that to a *kind* who'd seen his parents cut down and killed by a car? "Once the alpacas eat the grass in that field, I must put them in another field so they can graze."

"Oh." Jacob lowered his eyes.

"But they'll be right there in the morning. Why don't

you get ready for bed? I'll put an extra toothbrush in the bathroom for you."

The boy nodded, his eyelids drooping. "Can we pray for my *onkel* first?"

"Ja." Nathaniel was actually relieved to hear him speak of Titus. The boy had said very little about his *onkel* since Esther left.

Kneeling by the side of the bed along with Jacob, Nathaniel bowed his head over his folded hands. He listened as Jacob prayed for his *onkel's* health and thanked God for letting him meet the alpacas. Nathaniel couldn't help grinning when the boy finished his prayers with, "Make the alpacas like me, God, cuz I sure like them."

Nathaniel echoed Jacob's amen and came to his feet. Telling the boy he'd be sleeping on the other side of the hall, he added that Jacob should call if he needed anything.

An hour later, after he'd washed the few supper dishes and put them away, Nathaniel closed his Bible and placed it on a small table in the living room. The words had begun to swim in front of his eyes. He went upstairs and peeked into Jacob's room. The boy was sprawled across the bed in a shaft of moonlight. He'd removed his shoes and socks but not his suspenders. One drooped around his right shoulder, and the other hung loose by his left hip. His shirt had pulled out of his trousers, revealing what looked like a long scar. A legacy of the accident that had taken his parents? He mumbled something in his sleep and turned over to bury his head in the pillow once more. Nathaniel wondered if the boy had nightmares while he slept or if that was the one time he could escape from the blows life had dealt him.

Nathaniel slowly closed the door almost all the way.

The evening had gone better than he'd dared to hope. He went into his own room. He left his door open a crack, too, so he'd hear if the boy got up or if someone came to the kitchen door.

He went to the bedroom window and gazed out at the stars overhead. Was Esther looking at the same stars now? Was her heart heavy, as his was, with worries for Jacob and his *onkel*? Was she thinking of Nathaniel as he was of her? Since she'd fallen into his arms at the ball game he'd found it impossible to push her out of his thoughts. Not that he minded. Not a lot, anyhow, because it was fun to think of her sparkling eyes. It was delightful to recall how perfectly she'd fit against him.

He shook the thought from his head. Remembering her softness and the sweet scent of her hair was foolish. No need to torment himself when holding her again would be wrong. He couldn't ignore how much she loved being with *kinder* and how impossible it could be for him to give her *kinder* of her own. He needed to put an end to such thoughts now and concentrate on the one dream he had a chance of making come true: being a success on the farm so it didn't have to be sold.

Esther had just arrived home from school when she heard the rattle of buggy wheels. She looked out the kitchen window in time to see Nathaniel drive into the yard. She went to greet him and Jacob. She hoped letting him skip school had been a *gut* idea.

The afternoon breeze was strengthening, and her apron undulated on top of her dress. Goose bumps rose along her bare arms. She hugged them to her as she rushed to the buggy.

From it, she heard Jacob ask, "Isn't this where Esther lives?"

"*Ja*" came Nathaniel's reply.

"Why are we coming here? I thought we were going to *Onkel* Titus's house?"

"We are."

Esther kept her smile in place as a wave of sorrow flooded her. Never had she heard Jacob describe Titus's house as his home. Did he see it as another temporary residence?

Calling out a greeting, she pretended not to have heard the exchange. She gave Nathaniel and Jacob a quick appraisal. Both appeared fine, so she guessed their first day together had gone well. That was a great relief, because last night she'd felt guilty for letting Nathaniel take on the obligation of the boy. More than once, she'd considered driving over to his farm and bringing Jacob to her family's house. She was glad to see it hadn't been necessary. At least, not yet.

"Any news about Titus's tests?" Nathaniel asked.

She shook her head, glad he'd selected those words that suggested the elderly man's condition wasn't too serious. "Nothing, and you know what they say."

"No news is good news?"

"Exactly." She motioned toward the bank barn. "Ezra put Gal and Sal on the upper floor. He wasn't sure how they'd be around his cows."

"Is it all right if they stay here a little while longer? We're on our way to Titus's house to get some of Jacob's clothes and other things."

Glancing at Jacob, who hadn't said a word, she replied, "I'll go with you, if you don't mind."

"No, of course we don't mind."

"Jacob?" she asked.

The boy nodded with obvious reluctance.

"Let me get my bonnet." She hurried into the house. After letting *Mamm* know where she was going, she grabbed her black bonnet and her knitted shawl. She threw the shawl over her shoulders and went outside to discover Nathaniel had already turned the buggy toward the road.

Jacob slid over, leaving her room by the door. As soon as she was seated and the buggy was moving, he began asking her questions about the alpacas. She was kept so busy answering his question that the trip, less than two miles long, was over before she realized it.

The buggy rolled to a stop by a house whose weathered boards were a mosaic of peeling paint. The front porch had a definite tilt to the right, and Esther wondered if it remained connected to the house. Cardboard was set into one windowpane where the glass was missing. However, the yard was neat, and the remnants of a large garden out back had at least half a dozen pumpkins peeking from under large leaves.

As they stepped from the buggy, Jacob ran ahead. Nathaniel motioned for Esther to wait for him to come around to her side.

He chuckled quietly. "Blame those questions on me. Yesterday, Jacob asked me a lot of things I didn't know about. I kept telling him to ask you the next time he saw you. I didn't think he'd ask you *all* the questions at once."

"I'm glad to answer what I can, and I'm glad you're here to hear as well, so I don't need to explain them again to you."

He pressed his hand over his heart and struck the

pose of a wounded man. "Oh, no! I didn't realize I was supposed to be listening, too."

"You should know anytime you're around a teacher there may be a test at the end."

He laughed again, harder this time, as they walked to the door where Jacob was waiting impatiently. When the boy motioned for them to follow him inside, Nathaniel's laughter vanished along with Esther's smile.

The interior of the house was almost impassable. Boxes and bags were piled haphazardly from floor to ceiling. Esther stared at broken pieces of scooters, parts from *Englisch* cars and farming equipment mixed in with clothing and books and things she couldn't identify. If there was any furniture beneath the heaps it was impossible to see.

She guessed they were in the kitchen, but there were no signs of appliances or a sink. Odors that suggested food was rotting somewhere in the depths of the piles turned her stomach. She pushed the door open again, knowing she couldn't reach a window, even if she knew where one was, to air out the house.

"My room is this way." Jacob gestured again for them to follow him as he threaded a path through the piles with the ease of much practice.

Esther looked around in disbelief. Softly, so her words wouldn't reach Jacob, she said, "I had no idea Titus Fisher was living this way."

"I don't think anyone did other than his nephew." Nathaniel's mouth was a straight line as he walked after the boy.

She hesitated, not wanting to be buried if a mountain of debris cascaded onto her. How could this house have become filled with garbage and useless items? Surely someone came to call on the old man once in a while. She needed to alert the bishop, because other elderly people who were alone might also be living in such deplorable conditions.

Titus couldn't come home to this. Isaiah had said the stroke was a bad one, and if the elderly man survived he would be in a wheelchair. The path from the kitchen was too narrow for one.

Taking a deep breath, Esther plunged into the house. Her shawl brushed the sides of the stacks as she inched forward. How was Nathaniel managing? His shoulders were wider than her own. When she saw him ahead, sidling like a crab, she realized it was the only way he could move through the narrow space.

"Having fun?" he asked as he waited for her to catch up with him.

"Fun? Why would you say that?"

He grinned. "It's like being an explorer in another world. Who knows what lurks in these piles?"

"Mice and squirrels, most likely. Maybe a rat or two. Cockroaches. Do I need to go on?"

"Where's your sense of adventure?"

"Gone."

"I noticed." His face was abruptly serious. Tilting his head and eyeing her as if trying to look within her heart, he said, "You used to see an adventure in everything around us. What happened?"

She didn't want to have this discussion with him, especially not now when Jacob should be their focus. She tried to push aside some of the stacked items so she could move past him. It was as useless as if she were shoving on a concrete wall.

"Esther, tell me why you've changed." His voice had

dropped to a husky whisper that seemed to reach deep inside her and uncurl slowly as it peeled away her pretense.

No! She wouldn't reveal the humiliating truth of how she'd been so eager for adventure that she'd gotten involved with Alvin Lee. How could she explain she was supposed to be a respectable daughter and teacher, but she'd ridden in his buggy while he was racing it? What would Nathaniel think of her if he learned how she'd tossed aside common sense in the hope Alvin Lee would develop feelings for her?

Because he reminded me of Nathaniel, who, I believed, was gone forever from my life.

Astonishment froze her. Could that be true? No, she had to be *ferhoodled*. If she wasn't mixed-up, it had to be because she was distressed by the state of Titus's house and knowing Jacob had been living here. That was why she wasn't thinking straight. It had to be!

Nathaniel was regarding her with curiosity because she hadn't answered his question. She raised her chin slightly so she could meet his steady gaze.

"What happened? I grew up," she said before turning and shoving harder on the junk. Items fell on others, and it sounded as if several pieces of glass or china shattered. The path widened enough so she could squeeze past him without touching him. She kept going and didn't look back.

Chapter Six

$\sim$

Esther followed Jacob up the stairs, which were stacked with boxes. She heard Nathaniel's footsteps behind her but didn't turn. She shouldn't have spoken to him like that. It had been rude, and her reply was sure to create more questions. She didn't need those.

The upper hallway was as clogged with rubbish as the first floor. Each room they passed looked exactly like the rest of the house until Jacob opened a door and led them into a neat room.

How often *Mamm* had chided her and her siblings throughout their childhoods to keep their rooms orderly! *Mamm* would have been delighted to see how well Jacob kept his room.

Was it something he'd learned from his own *mamm*, or did he keep the clutter out of his room to have a refuge from his *onkel*'s overpowering collection? She blinked back tears. Either way, it was another sign of a *kind* who'd lost too much and was trying not to let his true feelings show.

Speaking around the clog in her throat, she said, "The

first things we're going to need are some bags or a *gut-*sized box."

"I think I know where I can find a box." Nathaniel grinned.

Jacob stepped in front of him to keep him from leaving the room. The boy's eyes were wide with horror. "No! You can't use one of *Onkel* Titus's boxes. Nobody touches anything in *Onkel* Titus's house but *Onkel* Titus."

"Not even you?" asked Esther gently.

The boy shook his head, his expression grim. "I did once, and I got the switch out behind the well house. I learned when *Onkel* Titus says something he means it."

Nathaniel glanced at her over the boy's head, and she saw his closely reined-in anger. A *kind* must learn to heed his elders, but that could be done gently. The idea of Titus striking Jacob for simply moving one of dozens of cardboard boxes set her teeth on edge, as well.

"Wait here." Jacob rushed from the room.

"No *kind* should live as he has here," Nathaniel said.

She squared her shoulders and took a deep breath. "We need to contact Reuben."

"The bishop—" He halted himself as Jacob sprinted into the room.

The boy tossed some cloth grocery bags on the bed. "We can use these. *Onkel* Titus says they're worthless. He'll be glad to get them out of his house."

"Gut." Esther kept her voice light. "Are your clothes in this dresser?"

"Ja."

"Pick out things other than clothes you want to bring and put them on the bed. Nathaniel and you can take them to the buggy." She counted. There were ten bags. "These should be enough to hold your things."

The boy faltered. "How long is *Onkel* Titus going to be in the hospital?"

Esther knew she must not hesitate. She didn't want to cause the boy more worry. "He has to stay there until the *doktors* tell him he can come home. I know you want him home right away, but it's better that the *doktors* are thorough so they know everything about your *onkel*'s health."

Jacob pondered that for several minutes, then nodded. "That makes sense."

"Don't forget your school supplies," she added.

"School?" He looked at Nathaniel. "I thought I didn't have to go to school while I was at your house."

"All *kinder* must go to school." Nathaniel grinned. "Nice try, though."

"When do I have to go back?"

"Monday will be early enough," Esther answered.

Jacob frowned, then began to gather his belongings. For the next ten minutes they worked in silent unison. Jacob set a few books, a baseball and his church Sunday black hat on the bed. Nathaniel put them into bags, making sure nothing was crushed. Esther packed Jacob's work boots and his best pair of shoes into another bag before turning to the dresser.

Like everything else in the room, the drawers were neat. Too neat for an eight-year-old boy.

When she mentioned that to Nathaniel while Jacob was carrying the first bags of clothing downstairs, he said, "Maybe it's his defense against the mess in the rest of the house. I'm glad we're getting him out of here." He picked up the last two cloth bags.

"Has he said anything about going to visit his *onkel*?"

"No."

"You'll let me know if he says something about going to the hospital, won't you?"

"Ja." He gave her a faint smile. "I'm sure he'll ask once he's less fascinated with the alpacas." Before she could add anything else, he asked, "Don't you think it's odd Titus wants to get rid of perfectly *gut* bags when he's stockpiling ripped and torn plastic ones?"

"Everything about him seems to be odder than anyone knows." She walked toward the door. "If I had to guess, I'd say Titus doesn't like cloth bags because you can't see through them. The plastic ones let him keep an eye on his possessions."

"How can he—or anyone else—see into the bags at the bottom of a pile?"

"You're being logical, Nathaniel. I don't think logic visits this house very often."

He led the way down the cramped stairs. When a board creaked threateningly beneath her foot, he turned and grasped her by the waist. He swung her down onto the step beside him. Her skirt brushed against the junk on the stairs. An avalanche tumbled loudly down the stairs and ricocheted off stacks on the ground floor. Things cascaded in every direction.

The noise couldn't conceal the sharp snap of the tread where she'd been standing. It broke and fell into the open space under the stairs.

Nathaniel's arm curved around her, pulling her away from the gap. Her breath burst out of her, and she had trouble drawing another one while she stood so near to him. When she did, it was flavored with the enticing scents of soap and sunshine from his shirt. With her head on his chest, she could hear the rapid beat of his heart. She put her hand on his arm to make sure her wobbly knees didn't collapse beneath her like the boxes and bags. His pulse jumped at her touch, and his arm around her waist tightened, keeping her close, exactly where her heart wanted her to be.

"Are you okay?" he whispered, his breath swirling along her neck in a gentle caress.

More than okay. She bit back the words before they could seep past her lips. At the same time, she eased away from him. Glancing at the hole in the staircase, she rushed the rest of the way down the stairs, past half-open bags spilling their reeking contents onto the steps.

She couldn't stay there with him. She'd been a fool to linger and let her heart overrule her head. Hadn't she learned that was stupid? Every time she gave in to her heart's yearnings for something it wanted—whether it was to let a much younger Nathaniel know how much he meant to her or to chase adventure with Alvin Lee— she'd ended up humiliated and hurt.

Esther hurried through the barely passable room, not slowing when Nathaniel called after her to make sure she wasn't hurt. She was, but not in the way he meant. It hurt to realize she still couldn't trust her heart.

Nitwit! Nitwit! Nitwit!

The accusation followed her, sounding on every step, as she found her way out of the horrible house. Fresh air struck her, and she drew in a deep, satisfying breath. Maybe it would clear her mind as well as her lungs.

Seeing Jacob trying to close the rear of the buggy, Esther went to help him. It took the two of them shoving down the panel to shut it after he'd squeezed the bags in there.

"All set," she said with a strained smile.

"If you say so…" His voice was taut, and she shoved her problems aside. "I don't think I need all that."

"If you're worried about Nathaniel making room for your things at his house, don't be."

Jacob surprised her by giving her a saucy grin. "I guess you've never been inside the house."

"I was years ago when I was about your age."

"That's a *long* time ago."

She smiled when she realized she was talking about a time before he was born. "Quite a long time ago. His *grossmammi* liked to quilt, so there were always partially finished projects in the living room."

"Not any longer. There wouldn't be room for a quilt!" He started to add more, then halted when Nathaniel pushed his way out of the house and gave the pair of bags to Jacob.

"These are the last of your clothes," he said. "You may have to hold them on your lap because I'm sure the storage area behind the seat is full."

"Let me check to see. I think I can fit these in there."

"Make sure the rear door closes. I don't want a trail of your things from here to Esther's house."

The boy smiled and opened the back. Bags started to spill out, but he shoved them back inside. Tossing the other two on top, he managed to close the door again.

Jacob chattered steadily on the way to the Stoltzfus farm. That allowed Esther to avoid saying anything. Nathaniel was, she noticed, as quiet, though he replied when Jacob posed a question to him. Unlike the swift ride to Titus Fisher's house, the one back seemed too long.

As soon as the buggy stopped in front of the white

barn, Esther jumped out. She was surprised when Nathaniel did, too. He told Jacob to wait while he hooked up the mules before Jacob drove the buggy to his farm. She'd assumed Nathaniel would tie the horse and buggy to the rear of his wagon.

"He'll be fine," Nathaniel said, and she knew her thoughts were on her face. "I've had him show me how he drives, and he's better than kids twice his age. From what he's told me, he's been driving his *onkel* to appointments with *doktors* and on other errands for the past six months or more."

She hesitated, then went with him into the barn. "Are you sure? I could drive him."

"Then we'll need to get you back here, and chores won't wait." He smiled. "I'll be right behind him, so he won't get any idea about racing my buggy. Not that he's foolish! The boy has a *gut* head on his shoulders."

His words silenced her. She'd thought she had a *gut* head on her shoulders, too, but she'd let herself get caught up in racing buggies on deserted roads late at night.

Nathaniel must have taken her silence for agreement because he went to the stall where the mules watched them.

As he led Gal out to the wagon, Esther asked, "Have you noticed Jacob never calls Titus's house his home? Only his *onkel*'s?"

"Now that you mention it, I have noticed that. I wonder why."

"He lost one home and one family." She watched Nathaniel put the patient mule into place, checking each strap and buckle to make sure it was right.

Straightening, he said, "Maybe he's afraid of losing another."

"That's sad. No *kind* should have to worry about such things."

"No *kind* should, but many don't have the happy and comfortable childhood you did, Esther." His mouth grew taut, and she got the feeling he'd said something he hadn't intended to.

"But he seems happier and less weighted down since you've taken him under your wing."

"Jacob has had too much sorrow and responsibility." Picking up the reins, he put his hand on the wagon's seat. "*Danki* for your help today, Esther. Let me know what Reuben says."

"I will." She drew in a deep breath, then said something she needed to say. Something that would be for the best for Nathaniel and for her. Something to prevent any misunderstandings between them. The words were bitter on her tongue, but she hurried to say, "I'm glad you're my friend. You've been my friend since we were *kinder*, and I hope you'll be my friend for the rest of our lives." She put her hand out and clasped his. Giving it a squeeze, she started to release it and turn away.

His fingers closed over hers, keeping her where she stood. She looked at him, astonished. Her shock became uncertainty when she saw the intensity in his gaze. Slowly, he brought her one step, then another toward him until they stood no more than a hand's breadth apart. She couldn't look away from his eyes. She longed to discover what he was thinking.

Suddenly she stiffened. What was *she* thinking? Hadn't she decided she needed to make sure he knew friendship was all they should share? She drew her arm away, and after a moment's hesitation he lifted his fingers from hers. At the same moment his eyes shuttered.

"Ja," he said, his voice sounding as if he were waking from a dream. Or maybe her ears made it sound that way because the moment when they'd stood face-to-face had been like something out of time.

"Ja?" Had she missed something else he'd said?

"I mean, I'm glad, too. We're always going to be friends." Now he was avoiding her eyes. "It's for the best."

"For us and for Jacob."

"Of course, for Jacob, too." A cool smile settled on his lips. "That's what I meant."

"I know." She took another step away. She couldn't remember ever being less than honest with Nathaniel before.

But it was for his own *gut*.

Right?

That's right, God, isn't it? She had to believe that, but she hadn't guessed facing the truth would be so painful.

"What a sad way for a *kind* to live!" *Mamm* clicked her tongue in dismay as she set her cup of tea on a section of the kitchen table where Esther wasn't working. "I don't know why none of us wondered about the state of the house before. An old bachelor and a young boy. Neither of them knows a lick about keeping a house."

Esther raised her eyes from where she was kneading dough for cinnamon rolls for tomorrow's breakfast. She'd added a cup of raisins to the treat she hadn't made for the family since spring. Now she chased the raisins across the table when they popped out as she folded the dough over and pressed it down. Dusting her hands with more flour so they didn't get stickier, she continued working the dough.

"Jacob never gave us any reason to think his *onkel* wasn't taking *gut* care of him." She beat the dough harder. "He comes to school in clean clothes, and he never smells as if he's skipped a bath."

"Don't take out your frustration on that poor dough." *Mamm* chuckled. "Don't blame yourself for not knowing the truth. None of us did, but now you have the responsibility of letting Reuben know."

"I plan to speak to Reuben. I'll go over once I get the bread finished." She was certain the bishop would know a way to help Jacob and his *onkel* without making either of them feel ashamed. She was as sure the *Leit*, the members of their district, would offer their help.

But where? At Titus's house or Nathaniel's? Jacob had mentioned in passing that the Zook farmhouse was as cluttered as his *onkel*'s. She was astonished. When she'd visited Nathaniel's grandparents during her childhood, the house had been pristine. In fact, he'd joked that no dust mote ever entered because it would die of loneliness. Sometime between then and now, the condition of the house had changed.

"Going to talk to Reuben is a *gut* idea," *Mamm* said, "but I don't think that's necessary."

"What?" Esther looked up quickly and flour exploded from the table in a white cloud. Waving it away, she said, "*Mamm*, we need to do something. Nobody should be living in there." *Or at Nathaniel's if it is also in such a sorry state.*

"You don't need to visit Reuben, because he just pulled into the dooryard."

"Oh." Esther punched the dough a couple more times

and then dropped it into the greased bowl she had ready. Putting a towel over it, she opened the oven she'd set to preheat at its lowest temperature. A shallow pan of water sat on the bottom rack, so the dough would stay moist in the gas oven. She put the bowl with the bread dough on the upper rack, checked the kitchen clock and closed the door. The dough needed to rise for an hour.

She began to wash the flour off her hands as her *mamm* went to the back door.

"Reuben, *komm* in," *Mamm* said. "We were talking about Esther paying you a call later today."

The bishop entered and took off the black wool hat he wore when he was on official business. He hung it on one of the empty pegs near *Mamm*'s bonnet. His gray eyebrows matched his hair and were as bushy as his long beard. He wasn't wearing the black coat he used on church Sunday. Instead he was dressed in his everyday work clothes, patched from where he'd snagged them while working on his farm.

"A cup of *kaffi*?" Esther asked as she took another cup from the cupboard. Everyone in the district knew the bishop's weakness for strong *kaffi*.

"Ja," he said in his deep voice. "That sounds *gut*."

She filled a cup for him from the pot on top of the stove. She set it in front of where he sat at the kitchen table where the top was clean. Taking her *mamm*'s cup, she poured more hot water into it before placing it on the table, as well. She arranged a selection of cookies on a plate for Reuben, who had a sweet tooth.

"Pull up a chair, Esther," Reuben said with a smile. When she did, he said, "Tell me how the boy is doing."

"He seems as happy as he can be under the circum-stances." She was amazed she could add with a genuine smile, "Jacob has fallen in love with the alpacas at Nathaniel Zook's farm, and they're pretty much all he thinks about."

"He needs to return to school."

"*Ja.* He'll be back on Monday. I wanted to give him a bit of time to become accustomed to the changes in his life. That also gives me time to work with the other scholars so they understand they need to treat him with extra kindness."

The bishop nodded. "An excellent plan. So tell me what you want to talk to me about."

"When we took Jacob to his *onkel*'s house, Nathaniel and I were disturbed by what we saw there." Esther quickly explained the piles of papers and boxes and everything anyone could collect. She told him about the narrow walkways through the rooms, even the bathroom. "The only place not filled to overflowing is Jacob's bedroom."

Reuben sighed and clasped his fingers around his cup. Letting the steam wash his face, he said, "I shouldn't be surprised. Titus is a *gut* man, but he's never been able to part with a single thing. I understand his *daed* was much the same, so the hoarding is not all his doing. *Danki*, Esther, for caring enough about the Fishers to want to help them. However, I'm not sure if we should do anything until we know what's going to happen with Titus. If it's God's will that he comes home, having his house cleaned out will upset him too much."

"How is he?" *Mamm* asked.

The bishop's face seemed to grow longer. "The *doktors* aren't optimistic. At this point, they can't be sure what his condition will be if he comes out of his coma. One told me he hadn't expected Titus to last through the first night, but he's breathing on his own and his heart remains strong. Is there anything of the man himself left? Nobody can know unless he awakens."

"Jacob will want to know how his *onkel* is doing," Esther said.

"Having the boy visit the hospital now might not be a *gut* idea. I'd rather wait until there's some change in Titus's condition before we inflict the sight of his *onkel*, small and ill in a hospital bed, on the boy."

"Can I tell him nothing's changed?"

"*Ja.*" He took a deep sip of his *kaffi*. "I don't like not telling Jacob the whole truth, but having him worry won't help."

Mamm stared down into her cup. "While we're waiting, we'll pray."

Reuben smiled and patted *Mamm*'s arm. "Putting Titus in God's hands is the best place for him."

"And Jacob, too," Esther said softly around the tears welling in her throat.

"And Jacob, too," repeated the bishop. "We'll need God's guidance in helping him as he faces the days to come."

Chapter Seven

Nathaniel ignored the chilly rain coursing down the kitchen windows as he tapped his pencil against the table. In front of him were columns of numbers he'd written. No matter how he added them, his expenses almost matched his income. The money from the rents on the fields was supposed to tide him over until he could bring in his own harvest next fall.

He wasn't going to have enough. He didn't want to start selling fields to keep from losing everything. If he sold more than one or two, he wouldn't have enough land to keep the farm going.

He could look for someone to loan him enough to get through the winter, spring and summer. Someone in Paradise Springs. He wouldn't ask his parents. They had money put away, but he knew they'd pinched pennies for years hoping his *daed* could retire from the factory in a few years.

There was another reason he couldn't ask his family for help. An unopened envelope sat on the table beside his account book. He didn't need to read it, because he knew his *mamm* was pleading with him again to return to Indiana where *doktors* would be able to help him if "the scourge" returned. He'd told her so many times that he hadn't needed to see an oncologist in six years. She refused to listen to the facts, still too shaken by what he'd gone through to believe the battle against his cancer had been won.

He pushed back his chair, something he was able to do now that he and Jacob had moved more of them into the barn. Leaning on the chair's two rear legs, he raked his fingers through his hair. There must be some way to keep the farm going until the fields produced enough that he didn't have to keep buying feed for the animals.

His *grossmammi* had bought the alpacas. Her mind had not been as muddled at the end of her life as his *grossdawdi*'s apparently had been. She'd intended the herd to be more than pets.

Hadn't she?

Looking across the kitchen, he stood. He paused when he heard footsteps upstairs. He was still getting accustomed to having someone else in the house, but he was glad Jacob was settling in well. Today would be the last school day he was skipping. On Monday, Nathaniel would have him there before Esther rang the bell.

Esther...everything led to her. When he'd held her close as the stair splintered, any thought of Esther the Pester disappeared as he savored the warmth of the woman she'd become. If she hadn't pulled away then— and again at her house—he wasn't sure if he could have resisted the temptation to kiss her. Just once. To see what it would be like. He should be grateful she'd stepped away, because when he was honest with himself, he doubted a single kiss would have been enough.

He couldn't kiss her when he couldn't offer to marry

her. Assuming she'd be willing to be his wife, he couldn't ask her. He'd first have to tell her the truth about his inability to give her *kinder*, and he didn't want to see pity in her expressive eyes.

Hochmut. Pride was what it was, and he wasn't ready to admit he wasn't the man he'd hoped to be: a man with dreams—no, expectations—of a home filled with *kinder*.

You could tell her the truth. His conscience spoke with his *grossmammi*'s voice. When he was young, she'd been the one to sit and talk to him about why things were right or wrong. Everyone else laid down the rules and expected him to obey them. Because of that, he shouldn't be surprised her voice was in his head, telling him that he was trying to fool himself.

Nathaniel grumbled under his breath. God had given him this path to walk. *Forgive me, Lord. You have blessed me with life, and I'm grateful.*

He went into the living room and to the bookcase next to his *grossmammi*'s quilting frame. Scanning the lower of the two shelves, he smiled as he drew out a thin black book. It was the accounts book his *grossmammi* had kept until she became ill. When he'd first arrived, he'd scanned its pages and seen something about income from the alpacas in it.

Returning to the kitchen table, he began to flip through it. His eyes narrowed when he noticed a listing for income from the alpacas' wool. He'd assumed they were sheared in the spring, and the dates of the entries in the account book confirmed that.

How did someone shear an alpaca? He'd seen demonstrations of sheepshearing at fairs, but had never seen anyone shear an alpaca. The beasts were bigger

and stronger—and more intelligent—than sheep. Three
factors that warned it'd be more difficult to shear them.

Jacob came into the kitchen and went to the refrigerator. He pulled out the jar of church spread and reached
for the loaf of bread.

"Hungry already?" Nathaniel asked.

"It's noon."

"Really?" Nathaniel glanced at the clock, startled to
see the morning had ended while he was poring over his
accounts…and thinking of Esther.

Closing the account book, he stuck his mother's letter in *Grossmammi*'s book to mark the page with the
entry about the alpacas' wool. He'd deal with writing
back to *Mamm* later, and he'd ask Esther about shearing the alpacas when he and Jacob attended services in
her district on Sunday.

"Do you want a sandwich?" asked Jacob as he slath-
ered a generous portion of the sticky, sweet spread on
two slices of bread.

Before Nathaniel could reply, a knock came at the
kitchen door. Who was out on such a nasty day? Dread
sank through him like a boulder in a pool. Was it Reuben or Isaiah with news about Jacob's *onkel*?

Please, God, hold Jacob close to You.

His feet felt as if they had drying concrete clinging
to them as he went to the door. He couldn't keep from
glancing at the boy. Jacob was moving his knife back
and forth on the bread, making patterns in the church
spread. The boy tried to look nonchalant, but Nathaniel
knew Jacob's thoughts were identical to his own.

*Be with him, Lord. He needs You more than ever
right now.*

Hoping no sign of his thoughts was visible, Nathaniel

opened the door. So sure was he that a messenger with bad news would be there that he could only stare at Esther. Her blue eyes sparkled with amusement, and it was as if the clouds had been swept from the sky. A warmth like bright summer sunshine draped over him, easing the bands around his heart, a tautness that had become so familiar he'd forgotten it was there until it loosened. Suddenly he felt as if he could draw a deep breath for the first time in more years than he wanted to count.

"Hi." Esther smiled. "We're here for a sister day."

"You want to have a sister day *here*?" Nathaniel's voice came out in a startled squeak as he looked past Esther, noticing for the first time that she wasn't alone. Behind her were two other women.

They crowded under the small overhang as they tried to get out of the rain. Each carried cleaning supplies, and he heard rain falling into at least one of the plastic buckets. Looking more closely, he realized one of the other women was Esther's older sister Ruth. She hadn't changed much because she'd been pretty much grown when he left Paradise Springs. She was more than a decade older than Esther and very pregnant.

He didn't recognize the younger blonde who was also several years older than Esther. When the woman smiled and introduced herself as Leah Beiler, he wondered why she was involved in a sister day with Esther and Ruth. He didn't want to embarrass her by asking.

"It's a school day," he managed to blurt out.

"Neva is teaching today. I decided I was needed here more than there."

"I don't understand."

"May we come in?" Esther asked, her smile never wavering. "I'll explain once we're out of the rain."

"Of course." He stepped aside so she and the other two women could enter. Hearing footsteps rushing into the front room, he knew Jacob was making himself and his sandwich scarce. Did the boy think his teacher was there to bring the schoolwork he'd missed?

"Do you remember Ruth?" Esther motioned for her sister to come forward. "She offered to help when she heard what I planned to do."

"Danki," he said, not sure why. It seemed the right thing to say.

Ruth, who resembled their *mamm* more than any of the other Stoltzfus *kinder*, nodded as she walked through the kitchen into the even more cluttered living room.

"Leah's already told you her name." Esther put her arm around the blonde's shoulders. "I don't know if you two ever met. The Beilers live on the farm next to ours." Without a pause, she went on, "We thought you could use a little help getting settled in here, Nathaniel."

Her sister grumbled, "It'll take more than a little help."

Esther ignored her and lowered her voice. "Jacob mentioned when we were at Titus's house that yours didn't look much better. I'm glad to see he was exaggerating."

"Not much." He put his hands on the backs of two chairs he'd pushed to one side. "My grandparents accumulated lots of things. I don't remember so many chairs when I came to visit."

"That, as Jacob reminded me the last time we talked, was a very long time ago. How were you to know what was going on while you were far away?"

Was she accusing him of staying away on purpose? When he saw her gentle smile, he knew he was allowing his own guilt at not returning to Paradise Springs while his grandparents were alive trick him into hearing a rebuke where there wasn't one. Except from within himself. For so long his parents had insisted he do nothing to jeopardize his health. He'd begun to feel as if he lived in a cage. The chance to try to make his dream come true had thrown a door open for him, and he'd left for Pennsylvania as soon as he could purchase a ticket.

"Where would you like us to start?" Esther's question yanked him out of his uncomfortable thoughts.

"You really don't need to do this. The boy and I are doing okay."

"I know we don't need to, but we'd like to."

"Really—"

He was halted when Leah smiled and said, "I've known Esther most of her life, and I can tell you that you're not going to change her mind."

"True." He laughed, wondering why he was making such a big deal out of a kindness. "I've noticed that about her, too."

"I'm sure you have." Leah chuckled before taking off her black bonnet and putting it on a chair. Instead of a *kapp*, she wore a dark kerchief over her pale hair.

Esther and her sister had work kerchiefs on, as well. He wasn't surprised when Esther toed off her shoes and stuffed her socks into them. She left them by the door when she picked up her bucket and a mop.

"You need a wife, Nathaniel Zook!" announced Ruth from the living room in her no-nonsense voice. "If you cook as poorly as you keep house, you and the boy will starve."

"I'm an adequate cook. Jacob is fond of church spread sandwiches."

Ruth rolled her eyes. "You can't feed a boy only pea-nut butter and marshmallow sandwiches."

"I know. Sometimes we have apple butter sandwiches, instead."

When her sister drew in a deep breath to retort, Esther interjected, "He's teasing you." She and Leah laughed, but Ruth frowned at them before she began pushing chairs toward the walls so she could sweep the floor.

Esther went to the sink. Sticking the bucket under the faucet, she started to fill it.

"You'll have to let it run a bit to get hot," he called over the splash of water in the bucket.

She tilted the bucket to let the water flow out. Holding her fingers under the faucet to gauge the temperature, she gave him a cheeky grin. "You need to have Micah come over and put a solar panel or two on your roof. You'll have hot water whenever you want it."

"Are you trying to drum up business for your brother?"

"You know how we Stoltzfuses stick together." She laughed lightly.

He did know that. It had been one of the things he'd first noticed about the family when he was young. Esther and her brothers might spat with each other, but they were a united front if anyone else confronted them. That they'd included him in their bond had been a precious part of his childhood in Paradise Springs.

Esther shooed him out of the kitchen so she and the others could get to work. He paused long enough to collect the sandwich Jacob must have made for him. Not wanting to leave the boy alone in the house with women determined to chase every speck of dirt from it, he called up the stairs. Jacob came running, and they made a hasty retreat to the barn.

"I hope they leave my things alone," the boy said when they walked into the barn and out of the rain.

"Don't worry." Nathaniel winked. "Your bedroom and mine should pass their inspection without them doing any work."

Jacob looked dubious, and Nathaniel swallowed his laugh. After he set the boy to work breaking a bale of hay to feed the horses and the mules, he went to get water for the animals. He stood under the barn's overhang and used the hand pump to fill a pair of buckets.

Hearing feminine laughter through a window opened enough to let air in but not the rain, he easily picked out Esther's lyrical laugh. He couldn't help imagining how it would be to hear such a sound coming from the house day after day. Listening to it would certainly make any work in the barn a lighter task.

"Hey, stop pumping!" cried Jacob from the doorway.

Nathaniel looked down to see water running from the bucket under the spout and washing over his work boots. He quickly released the pump's handle. Pulling the bucket aside, he sloshed more water out.

"Are you okay?" Jacob asked.

"Fine. Just daydreaming."

"About what?"

"Nothing important," he replied, knowing it wasn't a lie because what he'd been imagining wasn't ever going to come true. He needed to work on the dream he could make a reality—saving the farm from being sold. Otherwise, he'd have no choice but to return to Indiana and a life of working at the RV plant. He couldn't envision a much worse fate. He'd be stuck inside and never have the chance to bring plants out of nourishing soil.

And he wouldn't see Esther again.

He tried to pay no attention to the pulse of pain throbbing through him. Picking up the bucket, he walked into the barn. The boy followed, chattering about the alpacas, but Nathaniel didn't hear a single word other than the ones playing through his head. *You've got to make this farm a success.*

Esther wasn't surprised that the attic with its sharply slanting roof was filled with more chairs. What about them had fascinated Nathaniel's grandparents so much?

She wasn't sitting on one. Instead, she perched on a small stool so she could go through the boxes stacked beside her. Ruth and Leah had gone home an hour ago after leaving the house's two main floors sparkling and clean. Esther had remained behind, because she'd suspected the attic would be overflowing with forgotten things.

She'd found two baseball bats and a well-used glove that needed to be oiled because the leather was cracking. Jacob might put the items to *gut* use. In addition, she'd set a nice propane light to one side for Nathaniel to take downstairs, because it was too heavy for her to carry. If he put it by the small table in the living room, Jacob would have light to do one of the puzzles she'd stacked by the top of the attic stairs. As the weather grew colder and the days shorter, the boy would be confined more and more to the house.

Opening the next box, she peered into it with the help of a small flashlight. She wanted to make sure, before she plunged her hands into it that no spiders had taken up residence inside.

"Finding anything interesting?"

Esther glanced over her shoulder and smiled when she saw Nathaniel on the stairs. His hair was drying unevenly, strands springing out in every direction. He looked as rumpled and dusty as she felt, but she had to admit that looked *gut* on him. And she liked looking.

The thought startled her. Nathaniel was a handsome man, as he'd been a *gut*-looking boy. But she wanted his friendship now. Nothing more. She didn't want to make another mistake with her heart. It hadn't seemed wrong at the time when she discovered that Alvin Lee had loved racing. She'd been seeking an adventure. Exactly as Nathaniel was with his all-or-nothing attitude toward the farm.

She never again wanted the insecurity of wondering if the next dare to race a buggy or have a drink would lead to more trouble than she could get out of. Or of suspecting Alvin Lee might not be honest about being in love with her, despite his glib comments about how she was the one and only girl for him. Or of realizing, almost too late, how much her sense of her self-worth was in jeopardy.

No, she must not be foolish and risk her heart again.

She and Nathaniel must remain just friends.

Right?

She tightened her clasped fingers until she heard her knuckles creak. Why did she have to keep convincing herself?

Making sure she had an innocuous smile in place, she raised her eyes to meet Nathaniel's. "I've found a couple of useful things. I'm not sure I'd describe them as interesting."

"Useful is *gut*." He stepped into the attic but had to

bend so he didn't bump his head on the low ceiling. Glancing around, he said, "I've been meaning to come up here to sort things out since I moved back, but somehow the day flies past and I haven't gotten around to it."

"Where's Jacob?"

"In the barn. He's hoping to coax an alpaca to come to him. He's determined. I'll give him that."

"He's patient. One of these days, he'll succeed."

"If anyone can, it'll be him." Nathaniel looked into the box in front of her and grinned. Reaching in, he pulled out a pair of roller skates. He set the pairs of wheels spinning. "I remember these. *Grossdawdi* bought them for me when my parents refused to let us have roller skates. *Mamm* feared we'd break our necks—or get used to going fast so we'd never be content driving a buggy instead of a fast *Englisch* car."

"She thought you'd get what the *kinder* call the need for speed."

He laughed. "*Ja.* My grandparents kept the skates here and never told my folks about them, though I suspect *Mamm* grew suspicious when I returned home from visits too often with the knees on my trousers ripped. She never asked how I'd torn them, so the skates remained a secret."

"I remember you bringing them to our farm. You and my brothers used to have a great time skating in the barn."

"The only place smooth enough for the wheels other than the road, and your *mamm* wisely wouldn't allow us to play there." He set the skates on the floor beside the box. "Did you ever get a pair of your own?"

"I did. Hand-me-downs from one of my brothers, but I was thrilled to have them so I didn't have to walk to school in the fall and spring." She picked up one skate and appraised it. The black leather shoe wasn't in much better shape than the baseball glove, but with some saddle soap and attention it could be made useful again. "These look close to Jacob's size."

"I'll give them to him if you'll skate with us next Saturday."

"What?"

His eyes twinkled. "Don't pretend you didn't hear me promise your brother—our preacher—I'd make sure Jacob was kept safe. If I'm going to give him these skates, then we should make sure the boy has a place to enjoy them and someone to watch over him so he doesn't get hurt." He grinned. "I'll need someone to show me how to patch his trousers when he tears the knees out of them, too."

"You don't have any skates, do you?"

"I can get a pair. Does your brother sell them at his store?"

She shook her head. "Amos mostly sells food and household goods."

"There must be a shop nearby that sells them. I've seen quite a few boys and at least three or four men using Rollerblades to get around."

"Why don't you ask Amos? He usually knows where to send his customers for items he doesn't carry." She set the wheels on the skate spinning and grinned. "I used to love roller skating."

"Do you still have your skates?"

"Not the ones from back then. They were about the same size as these." She laughed as she held one against her foot. "My feet have grown since then. Besides, I don't skate any longer."

"Too grown-up?" he asked with a teasing smile, but she heard an undertone of serious curiosity in the question.

"Too busy to stay in practice."

He took the skate from her and set it next to the baseball bat. When he looked at her, his smile was gone. "I should have said this first thing. *Danki* for having your sister day here. I'm amazed at what you did downstairs in a few hours. Everything is clean, and many of the chairs are gone. Where did you put them?"

"Leah and I took most down to the cellar. We stacked the ones that would stack. The rest are out of the way behind the racks where your *grossmammi* stored her canned goods."

"*Danki*. That's a *gut* place for them until I can start donating them to mud sales in the spring."

"You may be able to get rid of them before then. Isaiah mentioned at supper last night that plans are being made for a community fund-raiser to help pay for Titus's hospital bills."

"I'd be glad to give the chairs to such a *gut* cause."

"I'll let him know."

He studied the attic again. "I should have known you'd be up here. You always liked poking around here when you and your brothers came over to play."

"Your *grossmammi* enjoyed having someone who'd listen to her stories about your ancestors who lived here long before she was born."

He squatted beside her. "Do you remember those stories?"

"A few."

"Would you share them with me?"

"Now?"

"No." His voice softened, drawing her eyes toward him. "Sometime when I can write down what you remember."

"You don't remember her stories?"

"I didn't listen." His mouth twisted in a wry grin. "I was too busy thinking of the mischief I could get into next to worry about long-dead relatives." His gaze swept the attic before meeting hers. "Now I'd give almost anything to hear her tell those stories again."

Her hand reached out to his damp cheek. He leaned against it, but his eyes continued to search hers. What did he hope to see? The answers to his questions? She doubted she recalled enough of his *grossmammi*'s stories to ease his curiosity.

"We learn too late to value what we have," he whispered. "By then, it may be lost to us forever."

Were they still talking about his *grossmammi*'s stories? She wasn't sure, and when he ran a single fingertip along her cheek, she quivered beneath his questioning touch. His finger slid down her neck, setting her skin trembling in anticipation of his caress. When his hand curved around her nape, he tilted her lips toward his.

A warning voice in her mind shouted for her to pull back, stand, leave, anything but move closer to him. She heard it as if from a great distance. All that existed were his dark eyes and warm breath enticing her nearer.

"Nathaniel, *komm* now!" Jacob exploded into the attic. He bounced from one foot to the other in his anxiety. Water pooled on the floor beneath him.

Esther drew away, blinking as if waking from a *wunderbaar* dream. She came to her feet when Nathaniel did. He glanced at her, but she looked away. She wasn't sure if she was more distressed because she'd almost succumbed to his touch or because they'd been interrupted.

Jacob's face was as gray as the storm clouds. What was wrong? She peered out the attic window. Through the thick curtain of rain, no other buggies were in sight, so Jacob couldn't have received any news about his *onkel*.

Nathaniel asked what was wrong in a voice far calmer than she could have managed, and the boy began to talk so quickly his words tumbled over one another, making his answer unintelligible. She thought she picked out a few phrases, but they didn't make sense.

...in the side of the barn...

...just missed...

Hurry!

The last he repeated over and over as they followed him downstairs and outside.

What had happened?

Chapter Eight

Wind-driven rain struck her face like dozens of icy needles, but Esther didn't return to the house for her bonnet or shawl. She ran to keep up with Jacob and Nathaniel. The boy didn't slow as he reached the barn. Throwing open the door, he vanished inside.

The interior of the barn was darker than the rainy day. Scents of hay and animals were thick, but not unpleasant. She blinked to get her eyes to adjust to the dimness, glad the roof didn't leak. Seeing Jacob rush through the door leading outside toward the pasture where the alpacas were kept, she swallowed a groan, ducked her head and followed.

The rain seemed chillier and the wind more ferocious. It tugged at her bandanna, and she put a hand on it to keep the square from flying off.

Looking over his shoulder, Jacob motioned for them to hurry. He ran toward the alpacas, for the first time not being cautious with them. The frightened creatures scattered like a group of marbles struck at the beginning of a game. At the far end of the field, they gathered together so closely they looked like a single multiheaded creature. Something must be horribly wrong for Jacob to act like this.

Her foot slipped on the wet grass, and she slowed to get her balance. Ahead of her, Nathaniel had caught up with the boy.

"Here! See it?" Jacob pointed at the side of the alpacas' shed.

She heard Nathaniel gasp. She ran faster and slid to a stop when she saw what the boy was pointing to.

An arrow! An arrow was protruding from the side of the small building. She choked on a gasp of her own.

Whirling, she ran into the shed. The steel point of the arrowhead protruded from the wall. She didn't touch it, knowing the point would be as sharp as a freshly honed razor.

She came back outside to see Nathaniel pulling the arrow out of the shed. He held it carefully and scanned the fields around the house and barn. She did, too, squinting through the rain trying to blind her.

"Where did it come from?" Nathaniel mused aloud.

"Probably a deer hunter," she said.

"They shouldn't be firing close to the alpacas."

She scowled. "I doubt it was *close* to the alpacas. More likely, someone was aiming *at* your herd. The light brown ones are fairly close to the color of a deer."

When Jacob cried out in horror, she regretted her words. Why hadn't she thought before she'd spoken?

"They don't have antlers, and they're not the same shape or size as a deer." Jacob looked at Nathaniel for him to back up his assertion.

She selected her words carefully, not wanting to upset the boy—or Nathaniel—more. "At this time of year, archers can shoot does as well as bucks. Irresponsible, over-eager hunters have been known to shoot at anything that moves. Ezra always has his Brown Swiss cows in a pasture next to the barn during archery season. Once the hunters can use guns, he brings the whole herd inside for the winter."

"You're joking." Nathaniel put his arm around Jacob's shoulders, and she noticed how the boy was shaking.

With fear or fury? Maybe both.

"No," she replied with a sad smile. "Some hunters shouldn't be allowed to hunt because they don't take the proper precautions when they're in the woods or traipsing across the fields. They ignore farmland posted No Trespassing. They're a danger to themselves and everyone else. Don't you remember how it was when you lived here years ago? Every fall someone loses a dog or some other animal because of clueless hunters."

"I remember."

"To be honest, we count ourselves blessed when no *person* is hurt or killed." With a sigh, she wiped rain out of her hair. "Right now, we need to check the herd and make sure none of them was hit. As frightened as they are, clumped together, it's impossible to tell if one is bleeding."

"Bleeding?" cried Jacob. "No!"

Nathaniel put his hand on the boy's shoulder. "Let's pray they're fine. But we need to check them. Do you remember how Esther got the alpacas into the shed?"

Jacob nodded.

"*Gut.* I'll need your help and Esther's, so we can examine them. They'll have to stay in until…" He looked at her.

"Until mid-December," she said. "I'm not exactly sure

when hunting season is over, but I can check with Ezra. He'll know."

"That's a long time," Jacob grumbled. "The alpacas like being outside."

"When they can come out again, it'll be nice and cool." Nathaniel smiled. "With their wool getting thicker, they'll be more comfortable then."

Jacob jumped to another subject with the innocence of a *kind*. He pointed to the arrow Nathaniel still held. "Can I have that?"

Nathaniel didn't wait for Esther to reply. Though she'd be cautious with the boy—after all, she seemed to be cautious with everything now—he didn't want to delay getting the alpacas into the barn. Not just the herd, but Esther and Jacob, too. The hunter might still be nearby and decide to try another shot at the "deer."

With a smile, he said, "I'll give you its feathers, Jacob. How's that?"

"Great!" His grin reappeared as if nothing out of the ordinary had happened.

"Let's get the alpacas inside first."

"Okay." He ran to get the two branches Nathaniel used to move the alpacas.

"Well done," Esther said quietly, and he knew she didn't want Jacob to overhear. "He can't hurt himself with feathers. If he had the arrow, he'd be sure to nick himself."

"I'll make sure it gets disposed of where no *kinder* can find it."

"*Gut.* There can't be any chance Jacob will decide to see if he can make it fly."

"As we would have?"

She scowled. "We were foolish *kinder* back then. I've learned it's better to err on the side of caution."

"You?" He began to laugh, then halted when she didn't join in.

"*Ja.* I don't know why you find it hard to believe."

He could have given her a dozen reasons, but she walked away before he could speak. Pushing his wet hair out of his eyes, he watched as she took the branches from Jacob and sent the boy running to open the barn door.

What had changed Esther so much? It was more than the fact that she'd grown up. He had, too, especially after facing cancer, but he hadn't lost his love of the occasional adventure. Yet whenever he hinted at fun, she acted as if he'd suggested something scandalous. What had happened to her, and why was she keeping it a secret?

Her shout for him to get inside with Jacob so the alpacas didn't see them spurred him to action. As he went into the barn, making sure the door was propped open, he saw the alpacas milling about, frightened and more uncooperative than they'd been since he'd arrived at the farm.

More quickly than he'd have guessed she could, she moved the herd into the pen at one side of the barn. He closed the door and dropped the bar, locking it into place so the alpacas couldn't push against the door and escape.

Esther moved among them, talking softly. She might be perturbed with him, but she was gentle with the terrified beasts. While she checked the alpacas in the center of the herd, he and Jacob walked around the outside, keeping the creatures from fleeing to the corners of the pen before she could look at them.

Nearly a half hour later, she edged out of the herd

and motioned for him and Jacob to step back. The alpacas turned as one. They rushed toward the door, halting when they realized the opening was gone. Moving along the wall, they searched for it.

"They'll calm down soon." Esther wiped her apron. It was covered with bits of wool and debris that had been twisted into the alpacas' coats. "Are you going to let the police know what happened?"

Nathaniel couldn't hide his shock because the Amish didn't involve outsiders unless it was a true emergency. "Why? Nobody was hurt."

"This time."

He shook his head. "I won't go to the police without alerting Reuben and my district's preachers first."

"Talk to them. No one was hurt this time, but someone fired off an arrow without thinking of where it could fly." She glanced at Jacob, who was watching the alpacas intently, but didn't speak his name.

There was no need. He understood what she hadn't said. Jacob was near the alpacas whenever he could be. A careless shot could strike him. Nathaniel needed to protect the boy who was his responsibility while his *onkel* was in the hospital.

As if the boy had guessed the course of his thoughts, Jacob asked, "Can I take the feathers and show them to *Onkel* Titus?"

This time, Nathaniel didn't have a swift answer. He thanked God that Esther spoke in a tone suggesting it was a question she'd expected, "As soon as the *doktors* say we can visit the hospital, you can take the feathers and tell your *onkel* about today."

"He'll be proud of me for not pulling out the arrow myself." The boy grinned.

"*Ja*, he will."

"He says no one should handle any weapon until they've learned how to use it the right way."

"Your *onkel* is a wise man." She returned his smile, and Nathaniel tried to do the same, though the expression felt like a gruesome mask.

"Because he's old." Jacob spoke with the certainty of his eight years. "He's had lots of time to learn." He pulled his gaze from the alpacas, which were already less frantic, and glanced over his shoulder. "That's what he tells me when I make a mistake or touch his stuff when I know I shouldn't."

Esther's smile grew taut, and Nathaniel gave up any attempt at one. Every time the boy mentioned his *onkel*'s obsession with those piles of junk, Nathaniel was torn between hugging the boy and wishing he could remind Titus that Jacob was more important than any metal or broken wood.

Jacob began to croon to the animals, but they wouldn't come closer to him. He whirled in frustration, his fists tight by his sides, and stomped his foot. At the sound, the alpacas turned and fled to the farthest corner of the barn. The boy's face fell from annoyance to dismay.

"Why don't they like me?" he asked.

Esther gave him a gentle smile. "They don't know you yet."

"I come out here every day. I help Nathaniel feed them. I make sure they have plenty of water. Why can't they see I won't hurt them?"

"Alpacas take a long time to trust someone. You have to be patient, Jacob."

"I have been."

"They still don't trust me completely," said Nathaniel,

"and I was taking care of them for more than a month before you came here."

Crestfallen, Jacob nodded. "I wish they liked me."

"If you give them time, they may," Esther said.

"I want her to like me." He pointed to a light brown female. "I want her to like me before she has her *boppli*."

"How do you know she's pregnant?"

"She told me." He grinned. "Not with words. I'm not out of my mind, no matter what other kids say. She told me by the way she looks. Like our dog did when she was going to have puppies."

"How is that?" Nathaniel asked.

"Her belly moves, and I know it's the *boppli* waiting to be born."

Esther patted Jacob's shoulder. "You're right, but you need to know one thing. Newborn alpacas are called crias."

"Why?"

"From what I've read, it's because the little ones make a sound like a human *boppli*. The word is based on a Spanish one, which explorers used when they first visited the mountains in South America where alpacas come from."

He nodded and said the word slowly as if testing out how it felt. "Cria. I like that. She's not the only one going to have a cria, is she?"

"I'd say there are at least five pregnant females."

"Are you sure?" Nathaniel looked from the boy to her. How would he ever make the farm a success if he'd failed to see something obvious to an eight-year-old boy?

"Not completely." Esther put her hand on the wall. "You should have Doc Anstine stop by and look at them.

He provided *gut* care for my alpacas, so he's familiar with their health needs."

Jacob grinned at Nathaniel. "Can I have one to raise by myself?"

"You need to see if the *mamm* alpacas are willing to let us near their crias."

"But if they will...?"

Nathaniel wanted to say *ja*, but he couldn't think of the alpacas and their offspring as pets. They might be the single way to save his grandparents' farm. On the other hand, he didn't want to crush Jacob's hopes.

Slender fingers settled on his sleeve, and he saw Esther shake her head slightly. How could what he was thinking be transparent to her, when he had no idea what secrets she was keeping from him?

You're keeping a big secret from her, too. His conscience refused to be silent, and he knew the futility of trying to ignore it. Now it was warning him of the dangers of ferreting out secrets better left alone.

"Let's talk about this later," Esther said, breaking into his thoughts. "Right now, will you watch the alpacas for Nathaniel?"

Jacob nodded, a brilliant smile on his face. "*Ja.* Maybe if they see me here, they'll know they're okay."

"You're right. What they need right now is what's familiar to them." She patted the boy's arm. "Stay with them ten or fifteen minutes, then come to the house. By the time you return later to make sure they're settled for the night, they should be fine. They may not know you kept them safe today, Jacob, but I know Nathaniel is grateful for your quick thinking."

"I am," Nathaniel said as the boy positively glowed. "The alpacas are important to me."

"Because they belonged to your *grossmammi*?" The boy hesitated, then reached into a pocket in his trousers. He pulled out a round disk. A yo-yo, Nathaniel realized. "This belonged to my *grossmammi*, and she gave it to my *daed* when he was a little boy. That's what my *mamm* told me." He stroked the wood that once had been painted a bright red. Only a few hints of paint remained. "My *onkel* owns a lot of stuff. He gave me some stuff of my own like my baseball and books. This is all I have that once belonged to my *grossmammi* and my *daed*."

The sight of the boy holding his single connection to the parents who had been taken from him by a drunk driver twisted Nathaniel's heart. Beside him, he heard Esther make a soft sound that might have been a smothered sob.

Knowing he must say something to the boy who had allowed them to see a portion of his pain, Nathaniel asked, "Do you always carry it in your pocket?"

"Not always." He shot a guilty glance at Esther. "I don't like others touching it, and I didn't know how much cleaning would be done in my room."

"Why don't you run and put it in your dresser drawer, so it doesn't get lost?"

"But the alpacas—"

"I'll stay here until you get back." He forced a grin. "I'll try not to upset them too much."

Jacob shoved the yo-yo into his pocket and bolted out of the barn.

By the pen, Esther wiped away tears she'd tried to hide from the boy. She gave Nathaniel a watery smile. "He'll be right back. I don't think he trusts you with *his* alpacas."

"I think you're right."

"FAST FIVE" READER SURVEY

Your participation entitles you to:
✳ 4 Thank-You Gifts Worth Over $20!

Complete the survey in minutes.

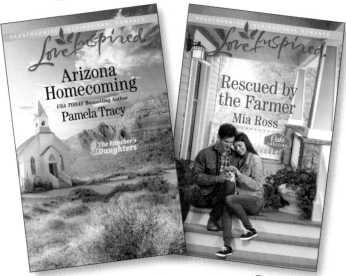

Get 2 FREE Books

Your Thank-You Gifts include **2 FREE BOOKS** and **2 MYSTERY GIFTS**. There's no obligation to purchase anything!

See inside for details.

Dear Reader,

Since you are a lover of our books, your opinions are important to us... and so is your time.

That's why we made sure your **"FAST FIVE" READER SURVEY** can be completed in just a few minutes. Your answers to the five questions will help us remain at the forefront of women's fiction.

And, as a thank-you for participating, we'd like to send you **4 FREE THANK-YOU GIFTS!**

Enjoy your gifts with our appreciation,

Pam Powers

To get your
4 FREE THANK-YOU GIFTS:

✱ Quickly complete the "Fast Five" Reader Survey
and return the insert.

"FAST FIVE" READER SURVEY

1 Do you sometimes read a book a second or third time? ○ Yes ○ No

2 Do you often choose reading over other forms of entertainment such as television? ○ Yes ○ No

3 When you were a child, did someone regularly read aloud to you? ○ Yes ○ No

4 Do you sometimes take a book with you when you travel outside the home? ○ Yes ○ No

5 In addition to books, do you regularly read newspapers and magazines? ○ Yes ○ No

YES! I have completed the above Reader Survey. Please send me my 4 FREE GIFTS (gifts worth over $20 retail). I understand that I am under no obligation to buy anything, as explained on the back of this card.

❏ I prefer the regular-print edition
105 IDL GKEV/305 IDL GKEV

❏ I prefer the larger-print edition
122 IDL GKEV/322 IDL GKEV

FIRST NAME

LAST NAME

ADDRESS

APT.#

CITY

STATE/PROV.

ZIP/POSTAL CODE

LI-816-SFF15

"He trusts you." She pushed away from the railing. Walking toward him, she said, "He showed you his most precious possession."

"And you, too."

She shook her head, and several light brown strands of her hair tumbled from beneath her kerchief. "No. If he trusted me, he wouldn't have put the toy in his pocket to make sure it was safe. Besides, I'm his teacher. You're his friend. He's learned he can depend on you."

"He'll come to see you're someone he can rely on, too." He stared at the long, damp curls along her neck. They appeared as silken as the alpacas' wool, and his fingers tingled at the thought of winding those vagrant tresses around them.

Pulling his gaze from them, he found his eyes lock with her pretty blue ones. They glistened with residual tears for the boy, but he saw other emotions, as well. Would she ever look at him with the longing he felt whenever she was close, a longing to hold her? Suddenly he found himself wondering if her eyes would close, brushing her long lashes on her soft cheeks, as he bent to kiss her.

No! He couldn't take advantage of her. She was unsteady in the wake of Jacob's confession...as he was.

He clasped his hands behind him before he pulled her close as he'd started to do in the attic before Jacob intruded. "One thing I can rely on is you. You're a *gut* friend, Esther Stoltzfus."

She didn't look at him as she said, "*Danki*. So are you." She stuffed her hair under her kerchief and headed toward the barn's main door. She didn't add anything else before she opened the door and was gone, leaving him more confused than ever.

* * *

When Nathaniel walked into Amos Stoltzfus's store, it was busy. Amos's customers hurried to get their errands and chores done before day's end. Tomorrow would be a day of worship, and no work, other than the necessary tasks of caring for farm animals, could be done.

In the midst of all the activity, Amos moved with a purposeful calm. He lifted a box down from a high shelf for an elderly man, who'd been standing on tiptoe to try to reach it on his own, though a pair of box grippers hung from a brad at the end of the aisle. He answered a *kind*'s question as if it were the most important thing he'd do all day.

Nathaniel smiled. There was no doubt Amos was a Stoltzfus. Not only did he have the brothers' height, something they didn't share with petite Esther, but he had the same sense of humor. He left everyone he spoke with either smiling or laughing. The Stoltzfus brothers seemed to have an ability to make others feel better... as Esther did, too. Nathaniel doubted any of them realized what a special gift they'd been given. It was simply a part of them.

"Nate—Nathaniel!" Amos grinned. "I'll get it right one of these days."

"As I told your *mamm*, it doesn't matter which name you use."

"What can I help you with?" He wiped his hands on his apron that was stained with a multitude of colors.

"I'm looking for roller skates." He'd planned to buy a pair last week, but the days had hurried past, each one busier than the preceding one. Between caring for his animals, trying to keep the house in some sort of order and taking Jacob to school, he hadn't had a second to call his own. Only because Neva, Esther's assistant teacher, had come over to the house today to help Jacob with the schoolwork he'd missed had Nathaniel been able to come to the Stoltzfus Family Shops alone. "Do you sell them?"

He shook his head. "You might try the bicycle shop on Route 30. It's not far from the post office. Someone told me they had a small selection. Otherwise, the closest place I know of is an *Englisch* shop near the Rockvale Outlets in Lancaster, and that'll take you about a half hour drive with heavy traffic each way. The *Englischers* are already swarming on the outlets for Christmas shopping."

"It's only October."

"I know." Amos shrugged and then chuckled. "Apparently they want bragging rights to being the first one done. Traffic is really hectic this time of year."

"Danki for the warning. I think I'll check the bicycle shop." He started to turn to leave, so Amos could assist his other customers. When Amos spoke his name, Nathaniel paused.

"Esther tells me the boy has settled in well at your farm. If you ever need some time to yourself, he's welcome to stay at our house."

"I know, but right now some stability is the best thing for him."

"If you change your mind—"

"Danki." He let a smile spread across his face. "But think about it, Amos. Would you have wanted to stay at your teacher's house?"

With a roar of laughter, Amos clapped him on the shoulder. "That's putting it in perspective." He was kept chuckling as he turned to help a woman Nathaniel didn't recognize find a particular spice she needed.

Nathaniel walked out, hoping he had enough time to get to the other shop and back to the farm before Neva had to leave. His life was hectic now, but he wouldn't have it any other way. He still needed to talk to Esther about shearing the alpacas so he could have cash to keep the farm going until next fall's harvest. If the alpacas' wool wasn't the solution, he wasn't sure where he'd turn next. He knew he couldn't return defeated to Indiana. Not only would his parents again smother him in an attempt to protect him, but he'd have to say goodbye to Esther.

He didn't want to face either.

Chapter Nine

The Sunday service was almost over. Esther saw two *mamms* with new *bopplin* slip back into the room. Little ones seldom could remain quiet for the full three hours of the service. The *mamms* had to inch through to sit among the other women because the church benches were closer together than usual. It was always a tight squeeze at the Huyard house.

Marlin Wagler, the district's deacon, stood to make announcements. First, as he did each church Sunday, he announced which family would be hosting the district's next service. Then he paused and glanced around the room.

Esther held her breath as the room grew so silent breathing would have seemed loud. This time of year there was an air of suspense during announcements. Secret engagements were made public along with letting the *Leit* know the couple's wedding date and who would be invited. She glanced around the room, trying to see who, besides her brother Ezra, wasn't there. When Ezra had stuttered over an excuse not to drive them to the Huyards' this morning, she'd guessed his and Leah's wedding plans were going to be published today. That was confirmed when Esther noticed Leah was missing, as well. It was traditional that an engaged couple didn't attend the service when their wedding was announced.

Anyone else?

Her search of the room came to an abrupt halt when her gaze was caught by Nathaniel's. Dressed in his Sunday *mutze*, he looked more handsome than usual. The black frock coat made his hair appear darker, something she hadn't guessed was possible. She noticed how the coat strained across his shoulders and guessed the hard work he was doing on the farm was adding to his already sturdy muscles.

She looked hastily away, not wanting anyone to notice how she was staring at him. But she couldn't keep from peeking out from beneath her lashes to watch him. He was scanning the rows where the women sat. Was he trying to figure out who was missing, too?

Or was he considering which single woman he might choose as a bride? That thought sliced through her like a well-honed knife, but she couldn't ignore the truth. He was in Paradise Springs to rebuild the family's farm. Why would he do that unless he planned to marry in the hopes of having a son to take over the farm when he was ready to retire? He needed someone who loved adventures and challenges, because she knew every day with him would be one.

That woman wasn't Esther Stoltzfus. When she told him she no longer roller-skated, Nathaniel had seemed to get the idea her days of seeking out adventures were in the past. Warmth crawled up her face when she recalled how the conversation between them in the attic ended. She shouldn't have touched him. That was too bold for the woman she wanted to be, but was it wrong to reach out when a friend was troubled? It was when thoughts of friendship had vanished as his fingers danced along her skin, setting it to sparkling like stars in a moonless sky. Then she'd watched his mouth coming closer to hers for a kiss.

In the open area between the benches, the deacon cleared his throat. The sound cut through Esther's reverie and brought her back to reality. A reality where she and Nathaniel were friends.

"Ezra Stoltzfus and Leah Beiler have come to me with their intention to marry," Marlin boomed over a *boppli*'s cries. "They've asked to be in our prayers, so please keep them in yours today and from this day forward."

Esther watched as *Mamm* stood to announce the date of the wedding. Her eyes were bright with tears, but Esther couldn't be sure if they were happy ones or if *Mamm* was thinking that it should have been *Daed* sharing the information today.

"Everyone is invited," *Mamm* said with a broad smile as she looked around the room, "no matter their age. Please pray the weather will be fine so we don't have to hold the wedding dinner in the barn."

That brought laughter from the adults and eager grins from the *kinder*. Many weddings restricted the age of the guests because there wasn't enough room for youngsters to be served along with the adults. Then some people couldn't attend because they had to stay home with the *kinder*.

Two other weddings were published, both for two days after Ezra and Leah's. There weren't enough Tuesdays and Thursdays, the days when the ceremonies were held, during the wedding season, so there were always conflicts. Esther was delighted there wouldn't be another wedding in their district on the day of her brother's wedding.

With a final prayer, the service came to a close. She went to the kitchen with half a dozen women to help serve the cold meats and sandwiches that had been prepared for their midday meal. The men and older boys rearranged the church benches as tables and seats for lunch. They would eat first, and then the women, girls and younger *kinder* would have their turn. The girls were watching the smaller kids run around while they got rid of some of the energy that had been bottled up during the long service.

Esther grinned as her *mamm* accepted *gut* wishes on the upcoming wedding. Volunteers came forward to promise to help with cooking and serving as well as cleaning up. Everyone enjoyed playing a part in a wedding, no matter how big or small the task might be.

By the time she'd eaten and helped wash the dishes, Esther suspected she'd heard about every possible amusing story of past weddings. She wiped her hands on a damp towel and went outside for some fresh air.

The afternoon was surprisingly balmy after the chill of the previous week. Not needing her shawl, she draped it over her arm as she walked toward a picnic table beneath a pair of large maples. In the summer, their broad branches offered shade for half the yard.

She sat, leaning against the table as she stretched out her legs. Hearing childish shouts, she smiled when she saw a trio of boys running toward the barn. Two were the younger Huyard boys, and the third was Jacob. He was joining in their game as if he always played with other *kinder*. They were laughing and calling to each other as they disappeared around the far side of the barn.

She closed her eyes, sending up a grateful prayer. Today, at least for now, Jacob was being a *kind*. It was a gift from God who was bringing him healing.

Even that simple prayer was difficult to complete, though it came directly from her heart, because her mind was filled with the work needing to be done before the wedding day. Perhaps Neva could fill in for her afternoons, so Esther could help *Mamm* and Leah and Leah's *mamm* get everything prepared. She'd been much younger when her oldest siblings married, and when her brother Joshua had wed for the second time earlier in the year it had been a simpler celebration.

Would it be her turn one day? She almost laughed at the question. When she considered the single men in the district, she couldn't imagine one she'd want to marry and spend the rest of her life with. Most of them thought of her as "one of the boys," as they had when they were *kinder*. They laughed with her and talked about the mischief they'd shared, but when it came time to select a girl to walk out with, they looked at the girls who'd spent their childhoods learning a wife's skills instead of climbing trees and racing across fields.

Was that why she'd fallen hard for Alvin Lee when he asked her to ride in his buggy the first time? He'd come to Paradise Springs about five years ago, so he hadn't known her as a *kind*. She'd been flattered by his attention, but when he raced his buggy she knew she should tell him she wanted no part of such sport. Instead she'd remained silent, telling herself she didn't want to look like a coward. The truth was she hadn't wanted to lose the one boy who might be able to look past her tomboy past.

She'd learned her lesson. It'd be better to remain a *maedel* the rest of her life than to offer her heart to someone who didn't want it. If she could find someone who could love her as she was…

Nathaniel's face filled her mind, but she pushed it away. He was risking everything on making his family's farm prosperous once again. Though she admired his dream, as she'd discovered with Alvin Lee, when a man focused obsessively on a goal—whether it was a successful farm or the best racing buggy in the county—everything and everyone else was dispensable.

She wouldn't let herself be cast off like the junk in Titus Fisher's house. Not ever again.

Nathaniel walked back from helping Jacob and the other boys set up a temporary ball field behind the barn. He saw Esther sitting alone at the picnic table. During the meal, she and Wanda had been asked question after question about the upcoming wedding. Esther had answered many of them, giving her *mamm* a slight respite.

Now she was alone.

He sat on the other end of the bench. It shifted beneath him, and her eyes popped open. She looked at him in surprise, and he wondered how far away her thoughts had been.

"Hiding?" he asked with a grin.

"In plain sight?" She half turned on the bench to face him, her elbow resting on the table. "Just thinking. Mostly about the things we need to get done before the wedding."

"Nobody seemed surprised by the announcement."

She chuckled. "It's hardly unexpected. I'm happy it's finally coming to pass."

"*Gut* things come to those who wait."

"I can't believe that's coming out of *your* mouth! You never were willing to wait for anything."

"Look who's talking!" He grinned. "Esther the Pester never waited for anything, either."

"Oh!" she gasped, her blue eyes widening. "I'd forgotten that horrible name! Don't mention it in front of Micah and Daniel. They'll start using it again."

With an easy grin, he said, "I won't, but it's not such a bad nickname."

"It is when you're trying to keep up with three older boys who sometimes didn't want you around."

"Not true." His voice deepened, and his smile faded. "I liked having you around, Esther. When I went to Indiana, you were what I missed most. Not my home, not my grandparents, not the twins. You."

"I missed you, too." Her gaze shifted, and he wondered what she was trying to hide. "You're here now, and you're helping Jacob. I saw him playing with the other *kinder*."

"I may have let him assume the alpacas might get along with him better if he could get along with his schoolmates."

"You didn't!" She laughed, the disquiet fading from her eyes. "Whatever he assumed, it's *gut* to see him acting like a normal *kind*."

Nathaniel grimaced. "Wouldn't a normal *kind* be curious about how his *onkel* is doing? It's been more than two weeks since Titus was taken to the hospital, and Jacob has barely expressed interest in going there. He speaks fondly of his *onkel*, so I'm surprised he doesn't want to see him."

"Don't forget Jacob was in the hospital for almost a month in the wake of the accident."

"I hadn't considered that."

"I don't know any way you could use his determination to have the alpacas accept him ease *that* problem."

He smiled, then said, "Speaking of the alpacas, what can you tell me about shearing them?"

"Only what I've read and observed. I've got a book at home that explains how an alpaca is sheared." She gave him a wry grin and folded her fingers on her lap. "Not that I ever attempted it myself. I took mine to a neighbor's farm when their sheep were sheared, and the men handled it when they were done with the flock. I let them keep the wool in exchange for their work. They seemed to think it was a fair exchange."

"How long did it take them to shear your alpacas?"

"Not long. Maybe ten minutes each or less."

"So quickly?" His hopes that the alpacas' wool might be the way to fund the farm until the harvest deflated. "I guess the wool isn't worth much."

"I didn't have enough to make it worthwhile to try to sell it on my own. With your herd of alpacas, you should be able to do well. This past spring, the best wool was selling for over twenty dollars a pound. The next quality level down sells for around fifteen dollars a pound."

He stared at her in amazement. "How do you know that?"

"I'd been thinking of getting a small herd of my own. Ezra has pastures I can use. I'd started collecting information about income and expenses, but I had to set it aside to begin the school year."

"You've never said anything about that."

"You never asked." She grinned the slow, slightly mischievous smile that always made his heart beat quickly.

"True." He tapped his chin with his forefinger. "I never guessed their wool would be so valuable."

"Alpaca's wool doesn't contain lanolin, so people who are allergic to sheep's wool can wear it. The cleaner the wool, the better price you can get for it."

"How do I keep it clean?"

"Some people put thin blankets over their alpacas to keep the wool as clean as possible."

"Like a horse's blanket?" He tried to imagine buckling a blanket around a skittish alpaca.

"*Ja*, but smaller and lighter. The covers have to be adjusted as the wool grows, so the fibers stay straight and strong."

"I should have guessed a teacher would have done her reading on this."

She raised her hands and shrugged. With a laugh, she rested her elbow on the table again. That left her fingers only inches from him. If he put his hand over hers, how would she react?

Stop it! he ordered himself. *How many more ways can she make it clear she wants to be friends and nothing more?*

"Looking up things in books is as natural to me as breathing," she said, drawing his attention from her slender fingers to her words. "I saw a bunch of books behind the chairs at your house. Could any of them help you?"

"I never noticed them until the chairs were moved, but I didn't find anything about alpacas."

"You're welcome to borrow the few I've collected."

"*Danki*. I—"

"Nathaniel! Esther! *Komm!*" called one of the Huyard boys. He, his younger brother and Jacob raced toward them, their faces alight with excitement.

The boy who'd shouted grabbed Esther's hand, and Jacob and the other boy seized Nathaniel's. Pleading with them to join in the softball game because the *kinder* needed more players, they tugged on the two adults.

She laughed and said, "You want us to play so you can strike me out again, Clarence."

The older boy grinned. "We'll take it easy on you."

"No, we won't," asserted his younger brother. "That wouldn't be fair, and we have to be fair. That's what you always say, Esther."

"*Ja*, I do. Milo is very, very serious about playing ball," Esther said with another chuckle as she stood. "Do you want to play, too, Nathaniel?" She held out her hand to him.

For a second, he was transported to the days when the Stoltzfus *kinder* had been his playmates. How many times had Esther stood as she was now, her hand stretched out to him as she asked him to take part in a game or an exploration in the woods or an adventure born from her imagination?

"Of course," he said as he would have then, but now it was because he wanted to see the excitement remain in her scintillating eyes.

When the two boys grabbed his hands again and pulled him to his feet, he walked with them and Esther to where other *kinder* were choosing teams. Soon the game began with Esther pitching for one side and he for the other. Nobody bothered to keep score as laughter and cheers filled the afternoon air.

One of the girls on his team hit a ball long enough

for a home run. When she ran around the bases and to home plate, he held up his hand to give her a high five. Instead she threw her arms around him and hugged him in her excitement.

"This is the best day ever!" she shouted.

"Ja," he replied, looking at where Esther was bouncing the ball and getting ready for the next batter. Her smile was warm as she urged her team not to get discouraged. When her gaze focused again on home plate, his eyes caught it and held it. Her expression grew softer as if it were especially for him. More to himself than the girl, he repeated, *"Ja.* It's a *gut* day. The very best day ever."

Chapter Ten

Esther had planned to go home from the Huyards' with *Mamm*, but stayed for the evening's singing when *Mamm* insisted she wanted some time to talk with Ezra and Leah about the wedding alone. They were waiting at the house.

"You'll be able to get a ride home with someone else," *Mamm* said, her eyes twinkling. "The Huyards have invited Jacob to stay with them and their *kinder* tonight, so Nathaniel doesn't have to bring him to school in the morning. Jacob is excited, and Nathaniel can have an evening without worrying about the boy. See how well that's working out?"

"Ja." She didn't add anything else. Telling *Mamm* to stop her matchmaking would be rude. Her *mamm* wanted all her *kinder* to be happily married.

She didn't want to be matched with Nathaniel. Right? Why did she keep thinking about riding in his buggy without Jacob sitting between them? The quiet night with only the sound of buggy wheels and horseshoes to intrude, a blanket over their laps to ward off the cold... his arm around her. She could lean her head against his shoulder and listen to his voice echo in his chest as he spoke.

She ejected those too-enticing thoughts from her mind. It'd be better if she just thought about the singing that had already started. From across the yard she could hear voices, which didn't sing as slow as during the church service. Going to a singing was the perfect way to end a church Sunday. As the weather worsened with the coming of winter, many singings would be canceled so people could get home before dark.

The barn doors were thrown wide open. Inside, propane lights set on long tables and on the floor sent bright light in every direction. A trio of tables to one side held snacks. Most of the singers had chosen a place on either side of the long tables. Couples who were walking out together sat across from each other so they could flirt during the songs.

Esther paused outside the crescent of light by the doorway, not wanting to intrude on the song. She wrapped her arms around herself as the breeze blew a chill across her skin.

"Are you going in or not?" asked Nathaniel as he stopped next to her.

"I could ask you the same thing."

"*Ja*, you could. They don't need me croaking like a dying frog in time with the music." He rubbed his right shoulder and grinned. "I'm not sure I want to show off how throwing a ball the whole afternoon for the *kinder* has left my shoulder aching."

"Only *half* the afternoon," she replied, wagging her finger. "The other half I was throwing the ball."

"You look as fresh as if you'd gotten a *gut* night's sleep. Don't rub it in."

She closed her eyes as the voices swelled out of the barn and surrounded them with "Amazing Grace." It was one of her favorite songs.

"You look pensive. Singings are supposed to be fun." He leaned against the wall by the door.

"Just listening," she said quietly. "A joyous noise unto the Lord."

"The hundredth psalm."

She nodded. "One of my *mamm*'s favorite verses, and whenever she reads it aloud, I imagine a grand parade entering the Lord's presence, everyone joyous and filled with music they couldn't keep inside."

"I know what you mean."

He did. He almost always had understood her without long explanations. Not once had he tried to make her into something she wasn't. When she looked at him, his face was half-lit by the lamps in the barn. His eyes burned through her, searing her with sweetness. He moved toward her.

She held her breath. His face neared hers, and she closed her eyes. Had time slowed to a crawl? What other explanation was there for his lips taking so long to reach hers? Her hands began to move toward his shoulders when someone stepped out of the barn and called to her.

Micah. If her brother discovered her about to kiss Nathaniel, she'd hear no end to the teasing.

Her eyes popped open. Nathaniel wasn't slanting toward her. Had she only imagined he intended to kiss her? Especially in such a public place with many witnesses? Perhaps she'd imagined his intentions in the attic, too.

As the song came to an end, Micah called, "Why are you loitering out here? The more the merrier." With a wave of his arm, he went inside.

Nathaniel glanced into the barn as dozens of conversations began among the singers. "Shall we go in? You can sing, and I can croak."

He must not have noticed her silly anticipation of his kiss. Doing her best to laugh at his jest, she walked in with him. The singers rose to help themselves to the cider and lemonade waiting among the snacks. In the busy crowd, she was separated from Nathaniel.

Esther thanked someone who handed her a cup of cider. She didn't notice who it was as she looked for Nathaniel. Not seeing him, she let herself get drawn into a conversation with Neva, Celeste Barkman and Katie Kay Lapp, the bishop's daughter. She realized Celeste and Katie Kay were peppering Neva with questions about Nathaniel.

"I don't know," her assistant teacher said in a tone that suggested she'd repeated the same words over and over. "Ask Esther. She's spent more time with Nathaniel and Jacob than I have."

The two young women whirled to Esther. She couldn't miss the relief on Neva's face. Katie Kay and Celeste were known as *blabbermauls*, and both of them fired a question at Esther. They exchanged a glance, then looked at her again...and both at the same time again.

Esther tried not to smile at the exasperated look they shot each other. Before they could speak a third time, someone clapped his hands and called for everyone to take a seat.

As the others rushed to the table, she drained the cup and put it beside others on a tray that would be returned to the kitchen later. She realized her mistake when she turned and saw Nathaniel at the far end with Katie Kay across from him and Celeste to his left. Katie Kay giggled as if what he'd said was the funniest thing she'd ever heard.

I doubt he's talking about alpacas with her. The ill-mannered thought burst through Esther's mind before she could halt it. Why was she acting oddly? Friendship was all she'd told Nathaniel they should share. It *was* all she wanted. Right? Right! If she ever offered her heart again, the man would be stolid and settled with the quiet dignity her *daed* had possessed. Watching Katie Kay flirt with Nathaniel made Esther's stomach cramp, as if she'd eaten too many green apples.

She looked away and saw her brother Micah leaning against some bales of hay by the snack tables. His arms were crossed in front of his chest and his face was blank. Except for his eyes. They narrowed slightly when Katie Kay giggled again at something Nathaniel said.

Esther had suspected for several months that her brother had a crush on the bishop's daughter, though, as far as she knew, Micah had never asked Katie Kay if he could drive her home from a singing. It wasn't easy to think of her jovial, outgoing brother as shy, but he was around the tall blonde. That, as much as anything, told her how much he liked Katie Kay.

Now the girl he liked was flirting openly with Nathaniel, his *gut* friend.

Walking over to him, Esther said, "Micah, if—"

"Everything is fine," he retorted sharply. "I want to stand over here. Okay?"

"Okay." She wasn't going to argue with him when she could see how distressed he was. "Do you mind if I stand here, too?"

"*Ja.*"

His answer surprised her, but she simply nodded before she took one of the last empty seats at the table. It was on the end of a bench with nobody sitting across from her. She smiled at the people sitting near her and joined in the singing as each new song was chosen. Her eyes swiveled from Nathaniel to Micah and back. Her brother was growing more dismayed, but Nathaniel was grinning as if he were having the best night of his life.

When the last song was sung, the pitchers were empty and the last cookie was gone, the participants stood. Some, including Esther, carried empty plates and cups to the house. The men hooked their horses to their buggies and waited for the girls who'd agreed to ride home with them. Though nobody was supposed to take note of who rode with whom, Esther knew hers weren't the only eyes noticing how Katie Kay claimed a spot in Nathaniel's buggy before he gave the command to his horse to start. Certainly Celeste saw, because she pouted for a moment before setting her sights on someone else. Soon she was perched on a seat and heading down the farm lane toward the main road, as well.

Esther stood by the barn door and watched the buggies roll away. Several of the men had mentioned how much their younger sisters and brothers had enjoyed playing ball with her, but not one asked if she needed a ride home.

Even Nathaniel, it seemed. She'd thought—twice— he was about to kiss her, but now he drove away with another girl. *Don't blame him for your overactive imagination.* She sighed, knowing her conscience was right.

"It looks as if we both struck out tonight." Micah jammed his hands into his pockets and frowned in the direction of the departing buggies. "I figured you'd ride home with Nathaniel."

"He didn't ask me." The words burst out of her before she could halt them.

"Oh." Micah put his arm around her shoulders and gave them a squeeze. "Let's go home."

She nodded, not trusting her voice.

The next evening, Esther was putting a casserole in the oven when the door opened. As she straightened, Leah Beiler entered. Leah wore a kerchief over her hair, and like Esther, her feet were bare. Her dress was black because she was still in mourning for her brother who'd died earlier in the year, but her eyes glistened with happiness. That, as much as the fact that Ezra was always whistling a cheerful tune, had been signs of how they'd fallen in love again after years apart, separated by miles and misunderstandings.

Would Esther offer her heart again to Alvin Lee if she had the chance? No! Not even if he put an end to his wild life and made a commitment to live according to the rules of the *Ordnung*. He needed to care about something other than drinking and racing. He must start looking toward the future.

As Nathaniel clearly was, because he'd asked Katie Kay to ride home with him. She shouldn't be bothered, but she was. Pretending she wasn't was lying to herself.

Help me remember what's best for both of us, she prayed.

She put a smile on her face. "Perfect timing, Leah. I can't make any other preparations for supper until after the casserole has cooked for half an hour. Would you like something to drink?"

"Do you have lemonade or cider?" asked Leah. "It's too hot for anything else."

"I know." Esther opened the fridge and took out a pitcher of cool cider. Moisture immediately formed on its sides and around the bottom when she set it on the counter. "It feels more like August than October."

Leah took two glasses out of the cupboard and picked up the pitcher, then gave Esther a shy smile because she'd acted as if she already lived in the farmhouse.

With a laugh, Esther asked, "If you hold that pitcher all afternoon, the cider will get warm."

"Oh, *ja*." Leah poured two glasses before handing Esther the pitcher.

She put it in the fridge. "Let's sit on the porch. Maybe there's a breath of air out there." She gave Leah another teasing grin. "And who knows? You might catch sight of your future husband."

"I like how you think."

Esther kept her smile in place by exerting all her willpower. If Leah had any idea of the course of Esther's endless circle of thoughts about Nathaniel and Katie Kay, she'd know Esther's teasing was only an act.

They sat on the porch and sipped their drinks. Few insects could be seen in the wake of overnight frosts the previous week, so there were no distractions as the sun fell slowly toward the western horizon.

Leah put her emptied glass on the floor by her chair. "Would you be one of my *Newehockers*? Unless Ezra has already asked you."

"He hasn't, and I'd be honored." The four attendants to the bride and groom needed to be available throughout the wedding day to help with everything from emotional support to running errands.

"Gut!" Leah's smile became bashful. "I can't believe this is finally happening."

"I can. Ezra never looked at another girl until you came back."

Leah flushed. "You shouldn't say such things."

"I'm only being honest."

"Esther, will you be as honest when I ask you what I have to ask you?"

"I'm always honest."

"Except when you think you might hurt someone's feelings with the truth. Don't deny it. I've seen you skirt the truth, though I've never heard you lie." She looked steadily at Esther. "Tell me the truth. Are you going to be okay with me taking over the household chores?" Before Esther could answer, Leah hurried on, "I know you've been in charge of the household since Wanda moved into the *dawdi haus*. Your brothers tell me what a *gut* job you've been doing."

"I'll be more than okay with you taking over the house."

"I'm glad that's cleared up. I didn't want to step on your toes."

She took Leah's hand and squeezed it. "Please feel free to step on my toes. I'll be glad to hand over anything you prefer to do yourself. It'll give me more time to focus on my scholars."

"How are the lessons going?"

"What do you mean?" she asked.

Leah's twinkling eyes warned she wasn't talking about school. She laughed. "Just teasing. How's Nathaniel doing with learning to take care of his alpacas?"

"I've taught him pretty much all I know until one of the pregnant females is ready to deliver. Once one of them has its cria, he'll know everything I know about them."

"I'm sure you'll find some other reason to visit the farm and make sure he's doing things right." With a wink, Leah stood. She picked up her empty glass and went into the house.

Esther didn't move. She should have been accustomed to the matchmaking now, and Leah hadn't been at the singing to see Nathaniel drive away with Katie Kay. Why hadn't Esther given her soon-to-be sister-in-law a teasing answer in return, as she had when Leah talked about taking over the household chores?

Because, she knew too well, she didn't care who did the cooking and cleaning, but she cared far too much about Nathaniel. The worrisome part was she didn't know how to change that.

Or if she wanted to, and that troubled her the most.

Nathaniel turned his buggy onto the lane leading to the Stoltzfus farm. Beside him, Jacob was almost jumping in his excitement and anticipation. The boy held his skates, the ones Esther had found in the attic, on his lap. He'd wanted to wear them in the buggy, but Nathaniel had refused. The boy could slip and fall getting in or out.

As he drew the buggy around the back of the house, he smiled. Esther was outside hanging up laundry. The clothes flapped around her in the gentle breeze, sending the fragrance of detergent spilling through the air.

She paused and looked around the shirt she held. Her eyes widened, and he knew she was surprised to see him and Jacob. After she finished pinning the shirt, she picked up the empty laundry basket and walked toward the buggy.

Nathaniel had already climbed out, and Jacob was

jumping down beside him, his roller skates thumping against its side.

"Ready?" Nathaniel called to her.

"For what?"

He heard the note of caution in her voice that never had been there when they were younger. What—or who—had stolen Esther's daring attitude? It couldn't be just growing up and becoming a teacher and wanting to be a role model for her scholars.

He lifted two pairs of Rollerblades out of the buggy. One was black and his perfect size. The other pair was a garish pink, the only ones he'd seen in what he guessed was her size. "It's past time to prove you've still got your skating skills. These should fit you."

"I've got some, too!" piped up Jacob.

Esther put the basket on the grass. Her gaze riveted on the bright pink skates. "Where did you find *those*?"

"At a sports store Amos recommended." Nathaniel grinned. "They didn't have any black or white ones in your size on the shelves, so I got these."

When he held them out to her, she took the Rollerblades, examining them with curiosity. "I've never used these kinds of skates."

"You've been ice skating, right?"

She nodded. "Years ago. The pond seldom freezes hard enough."

"This is supposed to be like ice skating."

"Supposed to be?" Her eyes widened again. "Don't you know?"

"I haven't tried mine yet."

She pressed the pink skates into his hand. "Let me know how it goes."

"You don't want to try?"

"Even if I did, those are so—so—"

"Pink?" He chuckled. "If it makes you feel better, get some black shoe polish and cover the color. We'll wait."

Jacob frowned. "I want to skate now. You said as soon as we got here, we'd skate."

Nathaniel motioned toward the boy with the hand holding the pink skates. "You heard him. Are you going to disappoint him because of the color of a pair of skates?" He leaned toward her. "Don't you want to try them?"

He could see she was torn as she looked from where Jacob sat on the buggy's step lacing on his skates. Maybe the daring young girl hadn't vanished completely.

She grabbed the basket and said, "Have fun." She started toward the house.

"I dare you to try them," he called to her back.

He half expected her to keep walking as she ignored his soft words. Esther the Pester wouldn't have been able to, but this far more cautious woman probably could.

When she faced him, he made sure he wasn't grinning in triumph. She wagged a finger toward him. "I don't take dares any longer. I'm not a *kind*."

"I can see that, but if you don't take dares, do you still have fun?"

"In bright pink Rollerblades?"

"Don't you at least want to try them?" He raised his brows in an expression he hoped said he was daring her again.

With a mutter of something he didn't quite get and knew he'd be wise not to ask her to repeat, she dropped the basket and snatched the Rollerblades out of his hand. She sat, pulling the skates onto her bare feet.

Nathaniel yanked off his workboots and secured his

skates tightly. He hadn't been ice-skating in years, but he remembered the boots needed to be secure or he was more likely to fall.

Esther stood beside him, rocking gently in every direction. She raised her arms to try to keep her balance. She almost fell when she laughed as Jacob couldn't stop before hitting the grass and dropped to his knees in it. The boy laughed, but Nathaniel's eyes were focused on her face.

It glowed with an excitement he'd seen only when she was playing ball with her scholars or working with the alpacas. This, he was convinced, was the real Esther, the one she struggled to submerge behind a cloak of utter respectability.

Why? he ached to shout. *Why can't you be yourself all the time?*

He didn't ask the question. Instead, he got to his feet. He took her hands and struggled not to wobble. The man at the shop had assured him anyone who had experience with ice-skating would have no trouble with inline skates. Nathaniel had had plenty of practice during the long, cold winters in Indiana. Now he wondered if the man had said that in hopes of making a sale.

As he drew Esther with slow, unsteady steps into the middle of the paved area between the house and the barn, he admitted to himself that the real reason he'd bought her the skates was for the opportunity to hold her hands as they had fun. She laughed when he struck the grass at the far end of the pavement and collapsed as Jacob had. Somehow she managed to remain on her feet.

Pushing himself back up, he dusted off his trousers. "You could have warned me how close I was to the edge."

"You could have found me skates that aren't bright pink." She folded her arms in front of her, but her scowl didn't match her sparkling eyes.

"I told you they were the only ones in your size."

"On the shelves. Did you ask what was stored in the back?"

He shook his head, unable to keep from grinning. "Probably should have."

"*Ja.* You probably should have." Her feigned frown fell away, and she chuckled. "Let's see if we can go a little farther."

She pushed off and was gliding across the pavement before he could grasp her hands again. With the skill she'd always had as a *kind*, she quickly mastered the Rollerblades and was spinning forward and backward.

More slowly, Nathaniel figured out how to remain on his feet. He doubted he'd ever be able to go backward, as she was, but he enjoyed skating with her and Jacob. The boy didn't seem to be bothered by his falls. He bounced up after each one, including one that left his trousers with a ripped knee.

"Someone's coming," called Jacob.

Nathaniel looped one arm around Jacob and another around Esther as a buggy came at a fast pace up the farm lane. He saw Reuben holding the reins. When Esther tensed beside him, he knew she'd recognized the bishop, too. There could be only one reason for Reuben to be driving with such a determined expression on his face.

"Esther," he began.

She didn't let him finish. Sitting, she began to unhook the bright pink skates as she said, "Jacob, let's go inside and get some cookies and cider."

"Are there any of your *mamm*'s chocolate chip cookies?"

"Let's see." She had the skates off and was herding the boy ahead of her toward the house by the time the bishop's buggy stopped next to Nathaniel's. She glanced back, and Nathaniel saw anxiety on her face.

Reuben didn't waste time with a greeting as he stepped out of his buggy. "I don't think we can wait any longer. The *doktors* are concerned because Titus seems to be taking a turn for the worse. They told me if the boy wants to see his *onkel* alive, he should come soon."

"We'll arrange for him to go tomorrow."

The bishop nodded, his face lined with exhaustion and sorrow. "*Danki*, Nathaniel. You and Esther have been a blessing for that boy." He glanced at the pink Rollerblades she'd left in the grass and smiled. "Though I can't say I would have approved of those if I'd been asked. *Gut* neither of you asked me." He turned to his buggy. "Let me know how the visit to the hospital goes."

"If Jacob wants to go."

Reuben halted. "You don't think he'll want to go?"

"He's been reluctant when I've asked him. Esther believes it's because he was in the hospital so long himself."

The bishop considered Nathaniel's words, then nodded. "We're blessed to have Esther as our teacher. She understands *kinder* well. Someday, she'll be a fine *mamm*."

Nathaniel must have said something sensible because the bishop continued on to his buggy. He had no idea what he'd said. Reuben's words were a cold slap of reality. *Ja*, Esther would be an excellent *mamm*. She deserved a man who could give her *kinder*. That couldn't be Nathaniel Zook.

The thought followed him into the house as he gently broke the news to Jacob, who was enjoying some cookies, that his *onkel* wasn't doing well. He didn't have details, because he realized he hadn't gotten them from Reuben.

"Do you want to go to the hospital to see your *onkel*?" he asked.

"Why can't I wait until he comes home? I hate hospitals!"

He looked over the boy's head to Esther whose face had lost all color. She comprehended, as the boy didn't, what it meant for the *doktors* to suggest he visit.

She sat beside Jacob. "I don't like hospitals either, but I think it's important you visit your *onkel*."

"Will you come with me, Esther?"

Surprise filled her eyes, and Nathaniel couldn't fault her. He hadn't expected Jacob to ask her to join them at the hospital that was on the western edge of the city of Lancaster.

She didn't hesitate. "If you want me to, I will."

Her response didn't surprise Nathaniel. Esther would always be there for her scholars or any *kind*. Another sign that he needed to spend less time with her because he was the wrong man for her.

So, why did life feel perfect when they were together?

Chapter Eleven

Esther didn't regret agreeing to go with Nathaniel and Jacob to the hospital, but that did nothing to lessen her dread about what they'd find there. In the weeks since Titus Fisher had his stroke, no *gut* news had come from the hospital. The reports she'd heard from Reuben and from Isaiah were the same—the old man showed no signs of recovery. His heart remained strong, but it was as if his mind had already departed.

She made arrangements for an *Englisch* driver, Gerry, to take them to the hospital the next morning in his white van. Also, she alerted her assistant teacher that Neva would be the sole teacher today.

When Gerry's van pulled into the farm lane, Esther hurried outside. The day promised to be another unseasonably warm one, so she didn't bring a coat or a shawl. She wore her cranberry dress and her best black apron. Beneath her black bonnet, her *kapp* was crisply pressed, and she wore unsnagged black stockings and her sneakers.

She watched while Gerry turned his van around so it was headed toward the road. The white van with a dent in its rear left bumper beside a Phillies bumper sticker was a familiar sight in Paradise Springs. The retired *Englischer*, who always wore a baseball cap, no matter the season, provided a vital service to the plain communities. He was available to drive anyone to places too far to travel to in a buggy. Also he'd drop passengers off and pick them up at the train station and the bus station in Lancaster. *Englischers* could leave their cars in the parking lot, but that wouldn't work with a horse and buggy. Though he claimed not to understand *Deitsch*, Esther suspected Gerry knew quite a few basic phrases after spending so much time with Amish and Mennonites.

"Good morning, Esther," he said when he opened the door to let her climb in. "It's good to see you again."

"How are you, Gerry?" She sat on the middle bench.

"Good enough for an old coot." He winked and closed the door as she pulled the seat belt over her shoulder. As she locked it in place, he slid behind the wheel. "Did your students like those colored pencils you bought for them before school started?"

"Ja." The *Englisch* driver had a sharp memory, another sign he cared about his passengers.

While Gerry chattered about baseball, his favorite topic even when the Philadelphia team wasn't in the playoffs, Esther sat with her purse on her lap and stared straight ahead. If she looked out the side windows at the landscape racing past at a speed no buggy could ever obtain, her stomach would rebel. She was already distressed enough about how Jacob would handle the upcoming visit. She didn't need to add nausea to the situation.

Gerry flipped the turn signal and pulled into the lane to Nathaniel's farm more quickly than she'd expected.

She took a steadying breath when the van slowed to a stop between the house and the barn. Glancing at the empty field where the alpacas had been, she wondered how they were faring inside. They'd be as eager to return outdoors as she was to have the visit to the hospital over.

As if he were bound for the circus rather than the hospital, Jacob bounced out of the house. He would have examined every inch of the van if Nathaniel hadn't told him that they needed to get in because Gerry might have other people waiting for a ride. As he climbed in, the boy noticed Gerry's Phillies cap. He edged past Esther and perched behind their driver. Nathaniel sat on the back bench and reminded Jacob to latch his seat belt. When she realized he didn't know how, Esther helped him.

Jacob peppered Gerry with questions about postseason baseball games as they drove to the hospital. Soon they were talking as if they were the best of friends, arguing the strengths and weaknesses of the various teams.

"How are you doing?" Nathaniel whispered from the seat behind her.

She turned to see him leaning forward. Their faces were only inches from each other. She backed away. Or tried to, because her seat belt caught, holding her in place. When he grinned, she did, as well. It would be silly to try to hide her reaction when it must have been obvious on her face.

"I'll be glad when this is over," she murmured, though she needn't have worried about Jacob. He was too enthralled with Gerry's opinion of the upcoming World Series to notice anything else.

"Me, too." His eyes shifted toward the boy. "He hasn't asked a single question."

She nodded, knowing he was worried about Jacob. She was, too. Jacob was holding so much inside himself. He must release some of it, or…she wasn't sure what would happen, but it couldn't be *gut* for the boy.

Neither she nor Nathaniel said anything else while the van headed along Route 30 toward Lancaster. When Gerry pulled into a parking lot in front of a four-story white building, she saw a sign pointing ambulances to the emergency room. She looked at the rows of windows that reflected a metallic blue shine, and she wondered if Jacob's *onkel* was behind one of them.

Gerry stopped in a parking spot that would have been shaded by some spindly trees in the summer. Now sunlight pushed past empty branches to spill onto the asphalt. He shut off the engine.

"When will you want to return?" Gerry asked, reaching to turn on the radio. The sounds of voices discussing the upcoming baseball games filled the van.

"We shouldn't be more than an hour," Nathaniel said.

"Take all the time you need. I don't have anywhere else to be the rest of the afternoon."

"Danki," he said, then quickly added, "Thank you."

"Anytime." Gerry folded his arms on the wheel and looked at where Jacob was staring at the hospital. "Like I said, take all the time you and the boy need."

Nathaniel got out first. Esther was glad for his help, and she had to force herself to relinquish his hand before they walked through the automatic doors. Jacob was delighted with how they worked with a soft whoosh, and she guessed he would have liked to go in and out a few more times. Instead, Nathaniel herded him toward a reception desk.

Esther followed. She was uneasy in hospitals, but

found them fascinating at the same time. People who came to them were often sick to the point of dying, and she despised how they must be suffering. On the other hand, she was impressed and intrigued by the easy efficiency and skill the staff showed as they handled emergencies and wielded the machinery that saved lives.

The receptionist looked over her dark-rimmed glasses as they approached. "May I help you?"

"We're here to visit Titus Fisher," Esther said quietly. "Can you tell us which room he's in?"

"Are you family?"

"Jacob is." She glanced at the boy who was watching people go in and out the doors.

"Let me see which room Mr. Fisher is in." She typed on the keyboard in front of her, then said, "Mr. Fisher is in the ICU."

Jacob, who clearly had been listening, frowned. "I see you, too, but what about my *onkel*?"

"ICU means the intensive care unit," Esther explained.

"Oh." The boy tapped his toe against the floor, embarrassed at his mistake.

"Don't worry, young man," the receptionist said with a compassionate smile. "We've got lots of strange names for things here. It takes a doctor almost ten years to learn them, and they keep inventing new ones."

That brought up Jacob's head. "*Doktors* are really smart, ain't so?"

"Very, so the rest of us can't be expected to know the words they use right away." Turning to Nathaniel and Esther, she said, "The ICU is on the third floor." She pointed to her right. "The elevator is that way. When you reach the third floor, follow the signs marked ICU."

"Danki," Esther said, and hoped the receptionist understood she was more grateful for her kindness than for the directions.

Nathaniel led the way toward where three elevators were set on either side of the hallway. He told Jacob which button to push, and the boy did, his eyes glowing with excitement as the elevator went smoothly to the third floor.

Jacob faltered when it came time to step out. Esther looked at him and saw his face was ashen. The full impact of where they were was hitting him. Did he remember similar hallways and equipment from his long stay in the hospital? She wanted to take him in her arms and assure him everything would be all right. She couldn't.

"Let's go," Nathaniel said, his arm draped around Jacob's shoulders.

When Jacob reached out and gripped her hand, Esther matched her steps to the boy's. She glanced at Nathaniel. His jaw was tight, and he stared straight ahead.

The ICU didn't have rooms with doors like the other ones they'd passed. Instead, one side of each room was completely open, so anyone at the nurses' desk could see into it. Some had curtains drawn partway, but the curtains on most were shoved to one side. Monitors beeped in a variety of rhythms and pitches. Outside each room, a television monitor displayed rows of numbers as well as the ragged line she knew was a person's heartbeat. Everything smelled of disinfectant, but it couldn't hide the odors of illness.

A nurse dressed in scrubs almost the exact same shade as the pink Rollerblades came toward them. "May I help you?"

"This is Jacob. He's Titus Fisher's great-nephew," Nathaniel explained.

Sadness rippled swiftly across the woman's face before her professional mask fell into place. "Follow me," she said. As she walked past the nurses' station, she explained to the other staff members the visitors were for Titus Fisher. When she continued toward the far end of the ICU, she added over her shoulder, "Usually we allow only two visitors at a time in here, but when children visit, we like having both parents here."

Esther opened her mouth to reply, then shut it. If the nurse discovered they weren't Jacob's parents, they might not be able to stay with him. She glanced at the boy. He was intently watching the monitors, his face scrunched as he tried to figure out what each line of information meant.

"Here you go," said the nurse as she pulled aside a curtain.

Stepping into the shadowed room, because there was no window, Esther looked at the bed. She'd rarely seen Titus as he seldom attended a church Sunday, but she hadn't expected to see him appearing withered on the pristine sheets. Tubes and other equipment connected him to bags of various colored solutions as well as the monitors.

Jacob's hold tightened on her hand. She winced but didn't pull away. He needed her now. When his lower lip began to quiver, Nathaniel put his arm around the boy's shoulders again. They stood on either side of him, and she guessed Nathaniel's thoughts matched hers. They wished they could protect Jacob from pain and grief and fear.

"Your *onkel* is asleep," she said in not much more than

a whisper. If she spoke more loudly, she feared her voice would break. She didn't want to frighten the *kind* more.

"He sleeps a lot," the boy said.

"This is a special kind of sleep where you can talk to him, if you want."

Jacob's brow furrowed. "What kind of sleep is that?"

Before she could answer, Nathaniel asked, "You know how you talk to the alpacas and they understand you, though they can't talk to you?"

The boy nodded, his eyes beginning to glisten as they did whenever the conversation turned to the alpacas.

"It's like that," Nathaniel said. "Right now, your *onkel* isn't able to answer you, but he can hear you. Why don't you talk to him?"

"What should I say?"

"You could tell him how much you love him," Esther suggested.

"That's mushy stuff." His nose wrinkled.

Esther smiled as she hadn't expected she'd do in the ICU. "Then tell him about the alpacas. That's not mushy."

The boy inched toward the bed and grasped the very edge of it. He was careful not to jar any of the wires or tubes, and he gave the IV stands a scowl. Again she wondered what he'd endured when he'd been in the hospital after his parents were killed.

"*Onkel* Titus," he began, "I got my stuff and took it to Nathaniel's, and some things fell into the hole when a stair broke. Otherwise, nothing's been touched. All your bags and boxes—except for the ones that fell in the hole—are there just as you like them."

He glanced over his shoulder at her and Nathaniel, then went on. "I'm staying with Nathaniel Zook. Do you remember him? He used to live in Paradise Springs when he was a kid. He's back now, and he's got alpacas!" The boy's voice filled with excitement as he began to outline in excruciating detail how he was helping take care of the herd and his efforts to get them to trust him.

Esther was glad for the shadows in the room so nobody could see the tears filling her eyes as she gazed at the boy who was brave and loving and compassionate. She wished she had his courage and ability to forgive. Maybe...

She kept herself from looking at Nathaniel. If things had been different. If things *were* different.

Things weren't different. He was walking out with Katie Kay, and he was her friend...just as she'd asked him to be.

But she knew it wouldn't be enough, and she'd thrown away her chance at love by ignoring her heart.

Nathaniel said nothing as he held the curtain open for Esther and Jacob. The boy was once again holding on tightly to her hand. Esther's taut jaw was set, and he couldn't ignore the tears shimmering in her eyes. He couldn't say anything about them, either. He didn't want to bring Jacob's attention to them or embarrass her in the ICU.

What he truly wanted to do was draw her into his arms and hold her until they both stopped shaking. Until he'd stepped into that room, he'd harbored the hope Titus would recover. Now he knew it was impossible. The elderly man hadn't reacted to anything while they were there, and Nathaniel knew that while Titus's body might be alive, his mind was beyond recovery.

In the elevator going down to the main floor, he

sought words to comfort Jacob and Esther. He couldn't find any. He wasn't sure there were any, so he remained silent as they walked out of the hospital and toward the white van.

Gerry must have read their faces because he got out and opened the doors without any comment. Jacob claimed the middle bench, and Esther sat with Nathaniel. As soon as they were buckled in, the van started for Paradise Springs.

They hadn't gone more than a mile before Jacob curled up on the seat. The emotions he hadn't shown in the ICU were like a shadow over him. When Esther began to talk to him, Jacob cut her off more sharply than Nathaniel had ever heard him speak to her. Shortly after, the boy fell asleep, exhausted from the visit.

Nathaniel turned to Esther whose gaze was focused on the boy. "*Danki* for coming with us," he whispered. "I wasn't sure how he'd handle seeing the old man."

As he did, she chose words that wouldn't intrude on Jacob's slumber. "He handled it better than either of us." Her voice caught. "He's too familiar with how quickly life can be snuffed out like a candle."

"Yet he knows when the old man dies, he'll have no place to go."

She faced him. "He does have a place to go. He's with you."

"He's welcome to stay at the farm for as long as he wishes, but he needs someone who knows how to be a parent. That's not me."

"You're doing a great job."

He gave a soft snort to disagree. "I depend on those witless beasts my *grossmammi* bought to keep him entertained. Otherwise, I don't know what I'd do. He's becoming more skilled with them than I'll probably ever be."

"You'd have managed to help without the herd."

"You've got a lot of faith in me."

"I do, but I also have a lot of faith God arranged for him to be at the best possible place when his *on*—the old man was taken to be monitored." She corrected herself with a glance at the boy. "God's plans for us are only *gut*."

This time, he managed to silence his disagreement. If God's plans for His *kinder* were only *gut*, then why had Nathaniel lost his hope of being a *daed*? He appreciated every day he'd been given, and he enjoyed having Jacob living with him in that big farmhouse. He was grateful the boy had found happiness as well as frustration with the alpacas. However, the boy was also a reminder of everything Nathaniel wouldn't have in the future.

Chapter Twelve

The day of Ezra and Leah's wedding dawned with the threat of clouds on the horizon, but by the time the service was over shortly before noon, the sun was shining on the bride and groom. Almost everyone in the district had come to the farm for the wedding, as *Mamm* had hoped.

After the service, Esther sat with her brother and new sister-in-law at a corner table among those set in front of the house. Everyone was excited to celebrate the first wedding of the season, especially one so long in the making. She smiled as she watched Ezra and Leah together. They were in love, and her brother had waited for ten years for Leah to return from the *Englisch* world. They deserved every ounce of happiness they could find together.

It was delightful to sit with them as food was served. Stories ran up and down the tables as the guests shared fond and fun memories of the newlyweds. Leah's niece Mandy and Esther's niece Debbie could barely sit still in their excitement, and more than one glass of milk was tipped over among the younger guests.

Mamm was just as happy. She'd had a broken arm and couldn't do much when Joshua, Esther's oldest brother, had married for the second time earlier in the year. She was trying to make up for that with Ezra's wedding as she talked to the many guests and made sure everyone had plenty to eat.

The day sped past, and Esther saw Nathaniel and Jacob in the distance several times. When she noticed Jacob joining other *kinder* for games in the meadow beyond the barn, she was relieved. She hadn't seen him since they went to the hospital. She'd agreed with Nathaniel that a few more days skipping school might help the boy. Now she was glad to discover he hadn't become traumatized and withdrawn again.

Jacob wasn't the only subject she wanted to discuss with Nathaniel, but she never had a chance to talk to him. During the afternoon singing, she'd been in the kitchen with *Mamm*, her sister and other volunteers while they washed plates from the midday meal and readied left-over food for dinner. The married or widowed women had urged her to join the singles for the singing, but she'd demurred after seeing Nathaniel walk into the barn with Katie Kay and Celeste. She didn't want to watch him flirting with them while they flirted with him.

Now the guests were leaving, and she hadn't even said hello to him. She stepped out of the kitchen and huddled into her shawl as the breeze struck her face. It was going to be cold tonight. Looking around the yard, she spotted several men standing near the barn where the buggies were parked.

Through the darkness, she could pick out Nathaniel. Her gaze riveted on him as if a beam of light shone upon his head. There was something about how he stood, straight and sure of himself, that always caught her eyes. Her heart danced at the thought of having a few minutes with him. Just the two of them. She waited for her conscience to remind her that friendship should be all she longed for from him.

It was silent, and her heart rejoiced as if it'd won a great battle.

Esther hesitated. Maybe she should stay away from him while her brain was being overruled by her heart. She might say the wrong thing or suggest she'd changed her mind.

But you have!

Ignoring that small voice of reason, she came down off the steps, but had to jump aside as a trio of young women burst out of the night. They were giggling and talking about the men who were taking them home. When she recognized them as Katie Kay, Celeste and her own cousin Virginia, she greeted them.

They waved with quick smiles, but were intent on their own conversation. Esther flinched when she heard Nathaniel's name, but she couldn't tell which one spoke it because they'd opened the door and the multitude of voices from the kitchen drowned out their words. She assumed it was Katie Kay. She squared her shoulders and crossed the yard. Clearly, if she wanted to speak with Nathaniel she needed to do so before he drove away with the bishop's daughter.

Again she faltered. Should she skip talking with him? No, she needed to know how Jacob was doing because he would be returning to school tomorrow. Because she was racked with jealousy—and she couldn't pretend it was anything else—didn't mean she could relinquish her obligations to her scholars.

The thought added strength to her steps as she left the house lights behind and strode toward the barn. She'd reached the edge of the yard when she heard a voice.

"Guten owed," said someone from the shadows.

Esther peered through the dark, wondering who'd called a "good evening" to her. Her eyes widened when Alvin Lee stepped out into the light flowing from the barn door in front of her. He hadn't attended church services or any other community function since the last time she'd spoken with him, the night she refused to be part of his reckless racing any longer.

There was no mistaking his bright red hair and his sneer. He used that expression most of the time. He had on the simple clothes every Amish man wore, but everything was slightly off. His suspenders had shiny clips peeking out from where he'd loosened his shirt over them. His hair was very short in the style *Englischers* found stylish and the faint lettering of a T-shirt was visible beneath his light blue shirt. She couldn't read the words, but the picture showed men wearing odd makeup and sticking out their tongues. She guessed they belonged to some *Englisch* rock-and-roll band.

She waited for her heart to give a leap as it used to whenever he appeared. Nothing happened. Her heart maintained its steady beat. She murmured a quick prayer of praise that God had helped it heal after Alvin Lee had turned his back on her because she didn't want to go along with his idea of fun and games.

"Heading toward the singing?" He leaned one elbow nonchalantly against the tree. He thought such poses made him look cool.

Cool was the best compliment he could give anyone or anything. In retrospect, she realized he'd never used it while describing her. Not that she needed compliments, then or now. They led to *hochmut*, something Alvin Lee had too much of. He was inordinately proud of his fancy buggy and his unbeaten record in buggy races. Though he'd never admitted it, she'd heard he'd begun wagering money with friends, Amish and *Englisch*, on his driving skills and his horse's speed. That would explain how he could afford to decorate his buggy so wildly.

"The singing was earlier today," Esther said, selecting her words with care. What did he want?

"Glad I missed it. Singings are boring, and nobody ever wants to sing music I like." He flexed his arm, and she saw the unmistakable outline of a package of cigarettes beneath his shirt. Smoking wasn't forbidden by the *Ordnung*, and some older farmers in the area grew tobacco, but it wasn't looked upon favorably, either. "I'm sure it was boring as death." He pushed away from the tree. "Attending singings is for the kids, anyhow. Why don't you come with me, and we'll have some real excitement?"

At last, she realized why he'd shown up after dark. He was looking for people to race with and drink with, and she didn't want to think what else he had in mind. She didn't want any part of it. Not any longer.

"I'm not interested." She turned to walk away.

He stepped in front of her again, blocking her way. "Hey, Essie, are you mad at me?"

"No." She didn't feel anger at him any longer. Nor did she feel special, as she used to when he called her by that nickname. She didn't feel anything but dismay at how he was risking his life for a few minutes of excitement.

"Are you sure? You act like you're mad." His ruddy

brows dropped in a frown. "Is it because I asked Luella to ride with me one time?"

"No," she answered, glad she could be honest when he wasn't. New reports of him and Luella riding together in his garish buggy were whispered almost every weekend. Esther had to be grateful that Alvin Lee hadn't decked out his buggy when *she* was riding with him. Otherwise, rumors would have flown about her and him, as well. "I'm not interested tonight."

"Sure you are, Essie. You've always been interested in fun."

"Not your kind of fun. Not anymore."

His eyes narrowed. "You're serious, aren't you?"

"How many different ways do I have to tell you I'm not interested?"

"They got to you, didn't they? Broke your spirit and made you a Goody Two-shoes."

She wasn't quite sure who "Goody Two-shoes" was, but the insult was blatant. "Nobody's broken my spirit. I've simply grown up." She flinched when she remembered uttering those same words to Nathaniel after they'd gone to Titus Fisher's house.

She hurried away, leaving Alvin Lee to grumble behind her. Relief flooded her. She'd spoken with him for the first time since he'd crushed her heart, and she hadn't broken down into tears or been drawn into being a participant in his dangerous races. Maybe she was, as she'd told him and Nathaniel, finally putting her childish ways behind her.

Esther heard him stomp away in the opposite direction. He hadn't pulled his buggy into the barnyard as the others had. With a shudder of dismay, she realized he'd cut himself off from the community as surely as Jacob once had. Would Alvin Lee see the error of his ways and reach out to others again as the boy was doing? Or was he too much a victim of *hochmut* to admit he was wrong?

She continued toward the barn. She wanted to talk to Nathaniel more than ever. She needed to listen to him. He didn't focus completely on himself. Even his idea of adventure was doing something important for his family, not something to give him a few moments of triumph over someone else.

As she neared the men, they were laughing together. She started to call out, but paused when she heard Nathaniel say, "Ah, I understand you now, Daniel. Playing the field is *gut* in more than baseball."

Her twin brothers roared in appreciative laughter before Micah replied, "Now there will be two of you leaving a trail of broken hearts in your wake."

"No, I wouldn't do that," Daniel said with a chuckle.

"No?" challenged Micah.

"No, and nobody seems to wonder if *I've* got a broken heart."

His twin snorted. "Because nobody's seen any sign of it."

"I like to enjoy the company of lots of girls, and they enjoy my company."

"Because they think you're serious about them." Micah's voice lost all humor. "I got a truly ferocious look this afternoon from Celeste Barkman until she realized I wasn't you, baby brother."

Nathaniel laughed along with Daniel before changing the subject to the upcoming World Series.

Esther knew she should leave. None of them had noticed her yet, and she shouldn't stand there eavesdropping. Yet, if she moved away, they would see her and realize she'd been listening.

The quandary was resolved when Nathaniel and her brothers walked toward the parked buggies. They didn't glance in her direction.

She turned and hurried toward the house. She was a short distance from the kitchen door when it opened, and Celeste and Katie Kay rushed out. They were giggling together as they told her *gut nacht*.

Thin arms were flung around her waist, and she smiled as Jacob hugged her.

"Are you leaving now?" she asked.

"*Ja*. Will you be coming to visit the alpacas soon?"

"I hope to."

"You could drive me home after school tomorrow, and you could see them then." He looked at her with expectation.

She hid her astonishment when he called Nathaniel's farm "home." Not once had he described Titus's place as anything other than his *onkel*'s house. It was a tribute to Nathaniel that the boy had changed. She was grateful to him for helping Jacob, but she shouldn't be surprised. Nathaniel had welcomed the boy as if he were a member of his own family from the very first. Though she was disturbed by how contemptuous Nathaniel had sounded about courting, she had to admit he'd done a *wunderbaar* job with Jacob.

Why had Nathaniel talked about playing the field as her brother Daniel did? She'd heard what sounded like admiration and perhaps envy in his voice at her brother's easy way with the girls.

"Esther?"

Jacob's voice broke into her thoughts, and Esther

smiled at the boy. "*Ja*. I'd like to check on the alpacas." She refused to admit she'd accepted the invitation so she could see Nathaniel without everyone else around to distract him.

"I'll tell Nathaniel!" With a wave, he ran toward where the buggies were beginning to leave.

Esther didn't follow. She stayed in the shadows beneath a tree as buggy after buggy drove past. Some contained families or married couples. Others were courting buggies, some with one passenger but most with two. Only one held three crowded in it: Nathaniel's.

She turned to watched Nathaniel's courting buggy head down the farm lane. From where she stood, she could hear Celeste's laugh drifting on the night air. That Jacob was riding with them, acting as a pint-size chaperone, didn't lessen the tightness in her chest or the burning in her eyes.

Nathaniel couldn't ask to drive Esther when she was already home, but why did he have to ask flirtatious Celeste, who hadn't made any secret of her interest in him? Why hadn't he spoken a single word to Esther all day?

Because you avoided him. Oh, how she despised the small voice of honesty in her mind! *Ja*, she'd found ways to stay away from him, but what would it have mattered if she'd shadowed him as Katie Kay and Celeste had? He was enjoying playing the field, an *Englisch* term for enjoying the company of many single girls. *And you told him you weren't interested.*

She'd been sincere when she said that, but was beginning to see her attempts to protect her heart by not risking it had been futile. Her heart ached now more than it had when Alvin Lee pushed her out of his life. God had led her away from that dangerous life, and she should be grateful He'd been wiser than she was. She was, but that did nothing to ease her heart's grief.

God, help me know what to feel. She longed to pray for God to give her insight into why Nathaniel had gazed at her with such strong emotions while they rode from the hospital…and days later blithely drove past her with another woman by his side.

Abruptly the night had become far colder—and lonelier—than she'd guessed it ever could.

Nathaniel turned his buggy onto a shortcut between the Barkman farm and his own. He hadn't planned to go so far out of his way when Jacob needed to be at school tomorrow. However, at this time of night, the winding, hilly road was deserted and the drive was pleasant. As the moonlight shone down on the shorn fields, he was alone save for his thoughts because Jacob was asleep.

He'd enjoyed the wedding more than he'd expected he would. Seeing friends whom he'd known as a *kind* had been fun, and he was glad they hadn't jumped the fence and gone to live among the *Englischers*. Several had married someone he never would have guessed they would. Time had changed them, and he knew they'd faced challenges, too, because they spoke easily of what life had thrown at them since the last time Nathaniel had visited his grandparents. Among the conversations that were often interrupted when someone else recognized him, nobody seemed to notice he said very little about his own youth.

He'd deflected the few questions with answers like, "Things aren't different in Indiana from here," or "Ancient history now. My brain is full of what I need to do at the farm. There isn't room for anything else." Both answers were received with laughter and commiserating nods, which made it easy to change the conversation to anyone other than himself.

However, he hadn't had a chance to spend any time with Esther. He'd known she'd be busy in her role as a *Newehocker*, but he'd hoped to have some time with her. She hadn't come to the singing, though he wouldn't have had much time to talk with her. The singing had gone almost like the one after church. Katie Kay Lapp had monopolized his time that day, not giving him a chance to speak to anyone else. At this afternoon's singing, she'd been flirting with a young man who was a distant cousin of the Stoltzfus family.

He'd been greatly relieved, until Celeste Barkman had pushed past several other people and lamented to him that her brother was going home with someone else and she didn't have a ride. As the Barkman farm wasn't too far out of his way, Nathaniel had felt duty-bound to give her a ride. He hadn't thought much about it until he happened to glance at the Stoltzfuses' house and saw Esther standing alone beneath one of the big trees.

She'd looked upset, though the shadows playing across her face could have masked her true expression. If she'd been disconcerted, was it because he was giving Celeste a ride? An unsettling thought, especially when Esther had stressed over and over she wanted his friendship and nothing more. Why wasn't she being honest with him?

Shouts came behind him, and Nathaniel tightened his hold on the reins. He'd been letting the horse find its own way, but the raucous voices were mixed with loud music coming toward him at a high speed. As Jacob stirred,

Nathaniel glanced in his rearview mirror. He was surprised not to see an *Englischer*'s car or truck.

Instead, it was a buggy decked out with more lights and decals than any district's *Ordnung* would have sanctioned. What looked like *Englisch* Christmas lights were strung around the top of the buggy, draped as if on the branches of a pine tree. He wondered how either the driver or the horse could see past the large beacons hooked to the front of the buggy. Twin beams cut through the darkness more brilliantly than an automobile's headlights. The whole configuration reminded him of decked-out tractor-trailers he'd seen on the journey from Indiana to Paradise Springs.

Who was driving such a rig? He couldn't see into the vehicle as it sped past him on the other side of the road, though they were approaching a rise and a sharp corner. Large, too-bright lights were set next to the turn signals at the back, blinding him. When he could see again, it was gone.

He continued to blink, trying to get his eyes accustomed to the darkness again. What a fool that driver was! He prayed God would infuse the driver with some caution.

"What was that?" asked Jacob in a sleepy tone.

"Nothing important. We'll be home soon."

"*Gut.* I want to make sure the alpacas' pen is clean before Esther comes tomorrow."

Nathaniel's hands tightened on the reins, but he loosened his grip before he frightened Bumper. The horse was responsive to the lightest touch.

Trying to keep his voice even, Nathaniel asked, "Esther said she was coming over tomorrow?"

"I asked her. She needs to check the alpacas."

"The veterinarian did."

Jacob yawned. "She knows more about them than Doc Anstine does."

Nathaniel had to admit that was true. She had a rare gift for convincing the shy creatures to trust her as she had with Jacob...and with him. He'd trusted her to tell him the truth, but he wasn't sure she had.

But you haven't been exactly honest with her, ain't so? Again his conscience spoke to him in his *grossmammi*'s voice.

He pushed those thoughts aside as his buggy crested the hill. He frowned. The flashy vehicle was stopped on the shoulder of the road. Slowing, he drew alongside it.

"Is there a problem?" he asked, bringing Bumper to a halt.

"Not with us." Laughter followed the raucous reply.

For the first time, Nathaniel realized that, in addition to the driver, there were a woman and two men in the buggy that had been built to hold two people. He wondered how they managed to stay inside when the buggy hit a bump. Two men were dressed in *Englisch* clothes, but he couldn't tell if they were *Englischer* or young Amish exploiting their *rumspringa* by wearing such styles.

"Nice buggy," the driver said. In the bright light, his red hair glowed like a fire. "It looks as if it were made by Joshua Stoltzfus."

"I guess so." He really hadn't given the matter any thought. It had been in the barn when he arrived at his grandparents' farm.

"He builds a *gut* buggy."

"I can't imagine any Stoltzfus not doing a *gut* job with anything one of them sets his or her mind to."

"Prove it."

Nathaniel frowned. "Pardon me?"

"Prove it's *gut*. We'll have a race."

He shook his head, aware Jacob was listening. "I don't want to race you."

"Scared I'll beat you?"

The driver's companions began making clucking sounds, something Nathaniel had heard young *Englischers* do when they called someone a coward.

"It doesn't matter why I don't want to race," he said, giving Bumper the command to start again. "I don't want to."

The outrageous buggy matched his pace. "But we do."

"Then you're going to have to find someone else." He kept his horse at a walk.

"We will." The driver leaned out of the buggy and snarled, "One other thing. Stay away from my girl."

He frowned. The red-haired man was trying to pick a fight, futile because Nathaniel wouldn't quarrel with him.

When Nathaniel didn't answer, the driver hissed, "Stay away from Esther Stoltzfus. She's my girl."

"Does she know that?" he retorted before he could halt himself.

The other men in the buggy crowed with laughter, and the driver threw them a furious glare.

"*Komm* on, Alvin Lee," grumbled one of the men. "He's not worth it. Let's go find someone else who's not afraid."

The buggy sped away, and Nathaniel wasn't sorry to see its silly lights vanish over another hill. Beside him, Jacob muttered under his breath.

When Nathaniel asked him what was wrong, Jacob

stated, "Racing could hurt Bumper. That would be wrong."

"Very wrong."

"So why do they do it?"

He shrugged. "I don't know. Boredom? Pride? Whatever the reason is, it isn't enough to risk a horse and passengers."

"Would you have raced him if I hadn't been here?"

"No. I'm not bored, and I know *hochmut* is wrong." He grinned at the boy. "I know Bumper is a *gut* horse. I know I don't need to prove it to anyone."

Jacob's eyes grew round, and Nathaniel realized the boy was startled by his words. He waited for the boy to ask another question, but Jacob seemed lost in thought. The boy didn't speak again until they came over the top of another hill only a few miles from home and saw bright lights in front of them.

"What's that?" Jacob pointed along the road.

Nathaniel was about to reply that it must be the redhead's buggy, then realized the bright lights weren't on the road. They looked as if they'd fallen off it.

"Hold on!" he called to Jacob. "Go!" He slapped the reins on Bumper.

As they got closer, he could see the buggy was lying on its side in the ditch. The sound of a horse thrashing and crying out in pain was louder than Bumper's iron shoes on the asphalt. He couldn't hear any other sounds.

After pulling his buggy to the side of the road, taking care not to steer into the ditch, he jumped out.

"Stay here, Jacob."

"The horse—"

"No, stay here. There's nothing you can do for the horse now."

The boy nodded, and Nathaniel ran to the broken buggy. He had to leap over a wheel that had fallen off. Pulling some of the lights forward, he aimed them within the vehicle. One look was enough to show him the two passengers inside were unconscious. Where were the others?

Running to his own buggy, he pulled out a flashlight. He sprayed its light across the ground and saw one crumpled form, then another. He took a step toward them, then paused at the sound of metal wheels in the distance.

Nathaniel looked past the covered bridge on a road intersecting this one. He saw another buggy rushing away into the night. Had it been racing this one? How could the other buggy flee when these people were hurt?

No time for answers now. He scanned the area and breathed a prayer of gratitude when he saw lights from an *Englisch* home less than a quarter mile up the road. He'd send Jacob to have the *Englischers* call 911.

He halted in midstep. He couldn't do that. The boy had seen his parents killed along a country road like this one.

Knowing his rudimentary first aid skills might not be enough to help now, he moved his own buggy far off the road. He told Jacob to remain where he was. Sure the frightened boy would obey, he ran toward the house. He hoped help wouldn't come too late.

Chapter Thirteen

Esther was on time for school the next morning, but several of her scholars were late. She guessed they'd stayed in bed later, as she'd longed to do. It hadn't been easy to face the day...and the fact Nathaniel had left with Celeste from the wedding. He seemed to be doing as he'd discussed with her brothers: playing the field.

She should be pleased he didn't include her in his fun and adventures, but it hurt. A lot. Alvin Lee had dumped her without a backward glance when she urged him to stop his racing. He'd called her a stick-in-the-mud, though he'd tried to convince her to join him again.

Telling herself to concentrate on her job, she looked around her classroom. Jacob wasn't at his desk. She wondered why he hadn't come to school. The other scholars were toiling on worksheets, and the schoolroom was unusually quiet.

Maybe that was why she heard the clatter of buggy wheels in the school's driveway. So did the scholars, because their heads popped up like rows of woodchucks in a field.

She rose and was about to urge the *kinder* to finish their work when the door opened. In astonishment, she met her brother Joshua's brown eyes. Whatever had brought him to the schoolhouse must be very important because he hadn't taken time to change the greasy shirt and trousers he wore at his buggy shop.

Her niece and nephew jumped to their feet and cried as one, *"Daed!"*

He gave them a quick smile and said, "Everything is fine at home and at the shop. I need to speak to Esther for a moment."

"Once you're done with your numbers," Esther said to the scholars, pleased her voice sounded calm, "start reading the next chapter in your textbooks. Neva and I'll have questions for you on those chapters later." She gave her assistant teacher a tight smile as a couple of the boys groaned.

Neva nodded, and Esther was relieved she could leave the *kinder* with her. Next year she wouldn't have that luxury, because Neva would have a school of her own.

As she walked to the door, Esther saw the scholars exchange worried glances. Apparently neither she nor Joshua had concealed their uneasiness as well as she'd hoped.

Her brother waited until she stepped out of the schoolroom and closed the door. She motioned for him to remain silent as she led him down the steps. He followed her to the swing set.

"Was iss letz, Joshua?" She could imagine too many answers, but pushed those thoughts aside.

"Alvin Lee is in the hospital."

She sank to one of the swings because her knees were about to buckle. Holding it steady, she whispered, "The hospital?"

"*Ja.* I thought you'd want to know." Joshua didn't meet her eyes, and she wondered how much about Alvin Lee courting her the family had guessed.

"What happened?" she asked, though her twisting gut already warned her the answer would be bad.

"He crashed his buggy last night while racing."

"How is he?" A stupid question. Alvin Lee would only be in the hospital if he was badly hurt. Otherwise, he'd be recovering at home.

"It's not *gut*, Esther. I don't know the details."

"What do you know? Was he alone?" The questions were coming from her automatically, because every sense she had was numb. Alvin Lee had wounded her deeply, but she'd believed she loved him.

"I know Alvin Lee is in the hospital because Isaiah was alerted and came to tell me before he left for the hospital. Luella Hartz was one of the passengers with Alvin Lee. She was treated in the emergency room and released to her parents. From what Isaiah heard, she's pretty badly scraped, and she has a broken leg and some cracked ribs. Two *Englisch* men were in the buggy, too, and they were banged up but nothing is broken." His mouth drew into a straight line. "The buggy was too small for four adults. No wonder it rolled when Alvin Lee couldn't make the corner. If a car had come along..." He shook his head.

Sickness ate through her. Alvin Lee had asked her to ride with him last night. If she had, she'd be the one with broken bones and humiliation. Or it could have been worse. She might be in the hospital, as Alvin Lee was.

God, danki *for putting enough sense in my head to save me from my own foolishness.* She added a prayer that all involved would recover as swiftly as possible.

"I hate to think of what might have happened if help hadn't arrived quickly," Joshua continued when she didn't reply. "They should be grateful Nathaniel went to a nearby *Englisch* house and called 911."

Her stomach dropped more. "Nathaniel? He was there?"

"Ja."

Esther wasn't able to answer. She felt as if someone had struck her. She couldn't catch her breath. Nathaniel? He'd been racing last night? With Alvin Lee? She was rocked by the realization she must have misjudged Nathaniel as she had Alvin Lee. Many times, Nathaniel had spoken of having a *gut* time. Was he—what did *Englischers* call it?—an adrenaline junkie like Alvin Lee?

Jacob had been with him. She asked her brother about the boy, but Joshua couldn't tell her anything. How could Nathaniel have been so careless? Blinding anger rose through her as she jumped to her feet.

"I want to go to the hospital and find out how Alvin Lee is doing," she said.

"They may not tell you." Joshua rubbed his hands together. "*Englisch* hospitals have a lot of rules about protecting a patient's privacy. When Tildie was in the hospital toward the end of her life, I had to argue with the nurses to let some of our friends come there to pray for her."

Esther blinked on searing tears. Though her brother was happy with his new wife and their melded family, the grief of those difficult months when his first wife had been dying of cancer would never leave him completely.

"I know they may not tell me anything, but I should go," she said.

"You know what you need to do, Esther." He gave

her a faint grin. "I know better than to try to stand in your way. From what Isaiah told me, Nathaniel is still at the hospital."

She glanced at the schoolhouse. "What about Jacob?"

"I don't know. Isaiah didn't say anything about him." He put his hand on her shoulder. "What can I do to help, Esther?"

"Call Gerry and tell him I need him to take me to the hospital as soon as he can. He can pick me up here."

"I'll call from the shop." He squeezed her shoulder gently, then strode away to his buggy.

Esther hurried into the school. She had a lot of things to go over with Neva before she left. If Gerry wasn't busy, his white van would be pulling up in front of the school shortly. She needed to be ready.

What a joke! How could she ever be ready to go to the hospital where Alvin Lee was badly injured? As well, she'd see Nathaniel to whom her heart desperately longed to belong…and who clearly wasn't the man she'd believed him to be. One fact remained clear—she had to be there for Jacob because she couldn't trust Nathaniel with him any longer.

Gerry's white van arrived in fewer than fifteen minutes. Esther knew she must have spoken to him on the trip to the same hospital where Jacob's *onkel* was. She must have made arrangements for him to take her home. She must have crossed the parking lot and entered the hospital and gotten directions to Alvin Lee's room. She must have taken the elevator to the proper floor and walked past other rooms and hospital staff.

All of it was a blur as she stood in the doorway of the room where Alvin Lee was. She resisted the urge to run away and looked into the room. Her breath caught as the beeping machines created a strange cacophony in the small room where the curtains were pulled over the window.

For a moment, she wasn't sure if the unmoving patient on the bed was Alvin Lee. She hadn't imagined how many tubes could be used on a single person. One leg was raised in a sling, and she saw metal bolts sticking out of either side. Each was connected to lines and pulleys. Bandages covered his ashen face except where a breathing tube kept raising and lowering his chest. Sprigs of bright red hair sprouted out between layers of gauze. That, as much as his name on the chart in the holder outside his room, told her the man who looked more like a mummy than a living being was Alvin Lee Peachy.

"Oh, Alvin Lee," she murmured, her fingers against her lips. "Why couldn't you be sensible?"

She received no answer as she walked to his bedside. She didn't expect one. A nurse, she wasn't sure which one because everything between her stepping into Gerry's van and this moment seemed like a half-remembered nightmare, had told her Alvin Lee was in what was called a medically induced coma. It had something to do with letting his brain heal from its trauma while keeping his heart beating. Everything else was being done for him by a machine or drugs.

She bowed her head and whispered a prayer. She'd have put her hand on his, except his had an IV taped to it.

Footsteps paused by the door, and she looked over her shoulder, expecting to see a doctor or nurse. Instead Nathaniel stood there. He was almost as haggard as Alvin

Lee. A low mat of whiskers darkened his jaw and cheeks, and his eyes looked haunted by what he'd seen.

Suddenly she whirled and flung herself against him. His arms enfolded her, and his hand on her head gently held it to his chest. Her *kapp* crinkled beneath her bonnet as he leaned his cheek against it.

The tears she'd held in flooded down her cheeks and dampened the black vest he'd worn to the wedding. Safe in his arms—and she knew she'd always be safe there—she could surrender to fear and sorrow. She remained in his arms until her weeping faded to hiccupping sobs.

"I'm done," she whispered, raising her head. "Where's Jacob?" She was caught by his wounded gaze, and she wished he'd free his pain as she had. She'd gladly hold him while he wept.

Esther stiffened and pulled away as she recalled what Joshua had told her. Nathaniel had been the one to call an ambulance last night. He'd been there when Alvin Lee was racing. Had they been competing against each other?

Nathaniel put his arm around her shoulders and drew her out of the room. The beeping sound of the machines followed them down the hall to a waiting area. After she'd entered, he followed, closing the door. She looked at Jacob who stood up from where he'd been sitting on what looked like an uncomfortable chair. He appeared as exhausted as Nathaniel, and she realized the boy had been at the hospital since last night.

Jacob threw his arms around her as he had after the wedding last night. Just last night? It seemed more like a decade ago now.

She hugged the boy and kissed his hair, which needed to be brushed. As she looked over his head toward Nathaniel, she had to bite her tongue to halt her furious words. How could he endanger this boy?

Nathaniel's brows lowered, but his voice remained steady as he said, "It was nice of you to come and see him, Esther."

"He didn't know I was there."

"According to his parents, the *doktors* say he can hear us, but he can't speak to us right now."

"Like my *onkel*," Jacob said as he rocked from one foot to the other. "*Onkel* Titus can't talk to us because he's listening to God now. God knows what he needs more than any of us, including the *doktors*. He can't talk to us because it's not easy to listen to God and to us at the same time."

Her eyes burned with new tears. What a simple and beautiful faith he had! Nathaniel's eyes glistened, too, and she knew he was as touched by Jacob's words as she was.

Not looking away from her, Nathaniel said, "Jacob, you remember where the cafeteria is, don't you?"

"*Ja.*"

"Go and get yourself a soda." He pulled several bills out of his pocket. "There should be enough here for some chips, as well."

The boy grinned at the unexpected treat. When Nathaniel told him he'd stay in the waiting room with Esther, Jacob left.

"Go ahead," Nathaniel said. "Tell me what's got you so upset you're practically spitting."

"You."

"Me?" He seemed genuinely puzzled. "Why?"

"I thought you were smarter than this, Nathaniel. I thought you meant it when you said making the farm a success was the great adventure you wanted. And Jacob…how could you risk him?"

Anger honed his voice. "What are you talking about?"

"Racing! How could you race Alvin Lee when a *kind* was in your buggy? Was Celeste in there, too? Were you trying to show off for her?"

"I wouldn't ever do anything that might hurt Jacob or anyone else." His gaze drilled into her. "I thought you knew me better."

"I thought I did, too." Her shoulders sagged. "But when I heard how you were racing Alvin Lee—"

"I didn't race him! He tried to get me to, but I refused."

"I was told—"

"I was the one who went to find a phone to call 911? *Ja*, that's true, but it was because I was the first one to come upon the accident." He dropped to sit on a blue plastic sofa. "After I told him I wouldn't race him, he took off. He must have found someone else to race because we came upon the buggy on its side only a little farther ahead. I don't know whom he was racing because the other buggy was more than a mile away on the far side of the covered bridge out by Lambrights' farm."

She sank to another sofa, facing him as she untied her bonnet and set it beside her on the cushion. "The other driver just left?"

"I told the police I saw a buggy driving away beyond the covered bridge, and they're going to investigate. Of course, it could be someone who wasn't involved. Maybe Alvin Lee was simply driving too fast."

"No. He's too skilled a driver to make such a mistake."

His brows lowered. "How do you know?"

"We all know each other in our district, Nathaniel."

"Be honest with me. You seem to have more knowledge of racing buggies than I'd thought you would."

Esther gnawed on her bottom lip. Why hadn't she kept quiet? She should have pretended she didn't know anything about the young fools who challenged one another.

He reached across the space separating them and took her hand. He clasped it between his. "I'm your friend, Esther. Tell me the truth about how you know so much about Alvin Lee's racing. Did you watch him?"

"Okay, if you want the truth, here it is." She doubted he'd think the same of her once she divulged what she'd hidden from everyone. "I know about racing. Not because I watched it, but because I was in buggies during races."

He pulled back, releasing her hands. "You could have been killed!"

"I wasn't. By God's *gut* grace, I know now, but at the time it was only meant to be a fun competition." She put up her hands when he opened his mouth to argue. "I learned it's dangerous. When I realized that, I didn't take part in any more races."

"Why did you start?"

Heat rose up her face, and she prayed she wasn't blushing. "Alvin Lee asked me to ride with him in one race. I didn't want to look like a coward."

"Oh."

Esther watched Nathaniel stand and walk toward the hallway. Was he looking for Jacob, or was he eager to get away from a woman who'd been silly?

"Is this why you're cautious about everything now?" he asked without facing her.

"I'm sure that's part of it. When we're young, we can't imagine anything truly terrible happening."

"Some do."

She waited for him to explain his cryptic comment. Silence stretched between them until the faint sounds from beyond the door seemed to grow louder and louder with each breath she took.

Slowly she stood. "Nathaniel, I was foolish, but please don't shut me out."

"I'm not shutting you out." He turned to look at her, his face as blank as the door behind him.

"No? I don't have any idea what you're thinking."

"You don't?" A faint smile tickled the corners of his mouth. "That's a change. You almost always have known what I'm thinking."

"I don't now. I wish I did."

He closed the distance between them with a pair of steps. Gently he framed her face between his work-roughened hands and tilted it as he whispered, "You're curious what I'm thinking? Do you really want to know?"

"Nathaniel—"

He silenced her as his mouth found hers. She froze, fearing she'd forgotten how to breathe. Then she softened against his broad chest as he deepened the kiss. She slid her arms up his back, wanting to hold on to him and this *wunderbaar* moment. All thoughts of being only his friend were banished from her mind as well as her heart.

He raised his head far enough so his lips could form the words, "*That* was what I was thinking. How much fun it would be to kiss you."

Fun? Was that all their kiss was to him? Fun? Another adventure? She didn't want to think of his jesting words with her brothers, but they rang through her mind.

Playing the field is gut *in more than baseball.*

"Esther…" he began.

The door opened, and Jacob came in. His grin was ringed with chocolate from the candy he'd been eating. He held a half-finished cup of soda in one hand and a crinkled bag of chips in the other.

"I should go," she said, grateful for the interruption.

She picked up her bonnet. If Nathaniel noticed how her hands trembled, he didn't mention it. Somehow, she managed to tell him and Jacob goodbye without stumbling over her words. She didn't wait to hear their replies.

What a mess he'd made of everything!

Nathaniel took off his straw hat and hung it by the kitchen door. The alpacas and the other animals were fed and watered and settled for the night. He checked the door out of the barn and the gate to the alpacas' pen to make sure they were locked. They constantly tested every possible spot to find a way out.

As Esther had at the hospital after he'd kissed her.

He couldn't guess why she'd retreated quickly, but he should be relieved she had. What had he been thinking to give in to his yearning to kiss her? A woman considered a man's kiss a prelude to a proposal, and he wouldn't ask her to be his wife. He cared about her too much—he *loved* her too much—to ask her to marry him when he couldn't give her *kinder*. The memory of one perfect kiss would have to be enough for him for the rest of his days.

God, You know I want her in my life. To watch her wed another man, knowing her husband will savor her kisses that set my soul alight, would be the greatest torment I can imagine.

He made himself a glass of warm milk and went into the living room, glad Jacob was upstairs. Sitting in the chair that had been his *grossdawdi*'s, he didn't light a lamp. Instead he stared out into the deepening darkness. It was silent save for the distant yapping of a dog. Not even the sound of a car intruded.

How could he stay in Paradise Springs where he'd see Esther and her husband and their *kinder*? He was realizing now that becoming a farmer and making his grandparents' farm a success had been in large part a cover for his desire to return to Lancaster County and to her. Something he hadn't realized himself until he understood he could have lost her forever in a buggy accident.

Should he give in to his *mamm*'s frequent requests and return home? He could sell the farm and the animals. Ironically, Esther would be his best chance of finding a home for the alpacas. She wanted a herd of her own. He couldn't imagine a better home for his animals—or for himself—than with her.

Stop it! Feeling sorry for himself was a waste of time and energy. The facts were unalterable.

Another thought burst into his head. *All you have to do is tell her the truth.* He needed to, because kissing her had changed everything. She might think he wanted to court her.

He did.

But he couldn't. Not without telling her the truth. He wasn't the man for her.

He needed to think of something else. He'd been shocked when she told him she'd taken part in buggy races. He wondered how many of those friends living a fast life she'd estranged when she came to her senses. Some important ones, he'd guess, by how dim her eyes had become as she spoke.

Abruptly he understood what she was *not* saying. One of those people who'd turned away from her must have been a suitor. It would explain why she'd lost much of her daring, turning into a shadow of the girl he'd known. She needed someone special to bring forth her high spirits again. Someone who understood Esther the Pester resided somewhere deep within her.

Someone like Nathaniel Zook.

He growled a wordless argument with his own thoughts, but halted when Jacob came down the stairs.

"Why are you sitting in the dark?" Jacob asked.

He held out his glass of lukewarm milk to the boy. "Sometimes a man likes to have some quiet time to think."

"*Onkel* Titus used to say that." Taking the glass, Jacob sat on the sofa. He swallowed half the milk in a big gulp.

"Your *onkel* sounds as if he's a very wise man."

"You'll see for yourself when he comes home from the hospital." Sipping more slowly, Jacob grinned. "I'm going to ask *Onkel* Titus if we can get some alpacas to raise on our farm. He's going to like them as much as we do, ain't so?"

Nathaniel let him continue to outline his plans for fixing his *onkel*'s outbuildings for alpacas and how he'd teach Titus what Esther had helped him and Nathaniel learn. There was no reason to dash the boy's dreams tonight, simply because his own had been decimated.

At last, Nathaniel said, "Time for you to get to bed, Jacob. You didn't sleep much last night, and you don't want to fall asleep while they're making cider tomorrow, do you?" Before the wedding, Jacob had told him about a trip the scholars were taking to a neighboring farm to watch windfall apples being squeezed into cider.

"No!" He jumped to his feet, ran out to the sink, rinsed out the glass and put it near the others to be washed after breakfast. With a cheerful wave, Jacob rushed up the stairs. His bedroom door closed with a distant click.

Nathaniel was left in the dark to try to figure out what he'd do and say the next time he saw Esther. As long as he was in Paradise Springs, he couldn't avoid her forever.

Chapter Fourteen

Nathaniel stepped out of his buggy and let the reins drop to the ground. Bumper would stay put until he returned. If the horse thought it was strange they'd returned to the place they'd left ten minutes before, he kept his thoughts to himself as he chomped on dried grass.

Hearing excited voices and a heavy metallic clunk, Nathaniel walked toward an outbuilding at the rear of the Gingerichs' farm where he'd been told the cider press was kept. The aroma of apples reached him long before he stood in the doorway.

Sunlight burst between the planks in the walls and seemed to focus on the large cider press in the middle of the barn. It was a simple contraption. Tall, thick wooden beams stood upright on either side. Stacked on a metal table with narrow gutters across it were planks with apples sandwiched between them. Heavier beams had been set on top of the uppermost plank and a heavy metal weight had been lowered onto them. From between the planks and running down the gutters to a hole in the side of the table were steady streams of the juice being squeezed out slowly by the weight.

Nathaniel noticed that in a single glance as his eyes adjusted to the dim interior of the barn. His gaze went to where Esther stood with her hands on the shoulders of two smaller scholars. She was making sure they could see the great press and the juice.

It'd been two weeks since he'd said more than hello or goodbye to her when he dropped off Jacob at school or picked him up at the end of the day. He'd known he would see her at services on Sunday if he attended in her district, but he hadn't made up his mind about going or not.

During that time, Alvin Lee Peachy had been released from the hospital into a rehab facility. The community was planning several fund-raising events to help pay for his care, which likely would continue for months, if not years. Nathaniel had seen flyers for a supper to be held next week as well as an auction after the first of the year. He planned to donate the extra furniture his grandparents had collected. If he did decide to sell the farm, the new owners wouldn't have to deal with the chairs.

But that wasn't the reason he'd returned to the Gingerichs' farm shortly after he'd brought Jacob to join the other scholars. He'd met the bishop on way home, and Reuben had shared news with him that he needed to deliver to Esther and the boy immediately.

He took a step into the barn, and Esther's head snapped up as if he'd pulled a string. Her smile evaporated. She bent to whisper to the two scholars beside her. Walking toward him, she caught her assistant's eye and pointed toward him and the door. Neva glanced at him and nodded.

Nathaniel went outside to wait for Esther. As she emerged from the barn, three apples in her hands, he saw wisps of cobwebs clinging to her dark blue dress. It was the same one she'd worn to her brother's wedding, and its color was a perfect complement to her eyes. His heart did somersaults, but he tried to ignore it.

"I thought you'd already left," Esther said in the cool, polite voice she'd used since the night he'd kissed her.

Not now, he ordered those memories that were both *wunderbaar* and sad. Squaring his shoulders, he said, "I did, but I have some news I didn't want you to hear from anyone else."

His face must have displayed the truth, because she clutched the apples close to her as she whispered, "Jacob's *onkel*?"

"He died this morning."

Tears rushed into her eyes, and he had to fight his hands that immediately wanted to pull her to him so he could offer her what sparse comfort there was. When she glanced at the barn, she asked, "What will happen to Jacob now?"

"I don't know." He swallowed hard. "I need to tell him."

"*We* will tell him. After school." A single tear fell down her cheek. "He's having such a *gut* time, and there's nothing he can do now, anyhow."

"I agree. Let him enjoy the day. I can stay here until…"

She shook her head. "No. We must make this seem like a normal day until we tell him what's happened. If you'd like to help—"

"You know I do."

"Bring Reuben with you," she finished as if he hadn't interrupted.

"*Gut* idea. I'll talk to him." He hesitated, wanting

to add that he needed to talk with Esther as well, to clear the air between them. He missed their friendship. How could a single kiss—a single splendid kiss meant to show her how much he cared for her—drive such a wedge between them? He hoped she wanted to recover their friendship as much as he did.

"Danki." She took a step back and wiped away her tears with the back of her hand. "I'll see you and Reuben after school."

He didn't have a chance to reply as she rushed into the barn. No sign of her dismay would be visible on her face when she was among the *kinder.* She'd make sure each of the scholars enjoyed the day. What strength she possessed! Exactly as she had when she was a little girl and kept up with and then surpassed him and her brothers. He'd loved her then, and his childish love had grown into what he wanted to offer her now.

Turning away, he went to his buggy. He'd drive to Reuben's farm and talk to the bishop before going to his own farm to tend to the animals. It was going to be a long, difficult day.

Esther didn't pretend to do work at her desk when the other *kinder* left after school. Jacob stood by a window and watched for Nathaniel's buggy.

"I'm sorry he's late," the boy said for the fourth time in as many minutes. "He's usually on time. Do you think the alpacas are okay?"

"I'm sure they're fine." It wasn't easy to speak past the lump filling her throat.

"What if one is having her cria?"

"Nathaniel knows you don't want to miss that."

"But—" He halted himself, then laughed. "Here he

comes now. He won't be able to tease me about being slow in the morning!"

She smiled, but her heart was breaking at the sight of his easy grin. Jacob had become a cheerful *kind* during his time with Nathaniel. Everything was about to change for the boy again, and she wished she could spare him the sorrow.

God, give us the right words and let him know we are here for him, though everyone in his family has gone away.

"Someone's with him," Jacob called from by the window. "It's Reuben. What's he doing here?"

"I'm sure he'll tell us."

"I haven't been fighting again. I'm being honest." His face flushed. "Most of the time, and always when it matters."

She put her arm around his shoulders. Was he trembling hard or was she? "Jacob, you know the bishop doesn't discipline members of our community. You don't need to worry, anyhow." She forced another smile. "You've been a very *gut* boy lately."

His shoulders drooped beneath her arm, and she realized how tense he'd been. She couldn't help recall how he'd mentioned his *onkel* punishing him harshly for the slightest transgression.

The door opened, bringing chilly air into the classroom. Reuben entered first, taking off his straw hat and hanging it where the scholars usually did. Nathaniel followed. As he set his hat on the shelf above the pegs, he looked everywhere but at her and Jacob. His face was drawn and looked years older than it had that morning. The day had been as painful for him as it had for her. Such news shouldn't ever be held as a secret within a heart because it burned like a wildfire, without thought or compassion.

She fought her feet that wanted to speed her across the room so she could draw his arms around her. She stayed where she was.

"Are the alpacas okay?" asked the boy before anyone else could speak.

"They're fine." Nathaniel gave him a gentle smile. "You can see for yourself as soon as we get there."

"Gut!" Jacob shrugged off Esther's arm and sprinted toward the door. "I'm ready. Let's go home now."

She saw the glance the two men exchanged, and she wondered if it was the first time they'd heard Jacob describe Nathaniel's farm as home.

Reuben cleared his throat. "Jacob, can we talk for a minute?"

"Ja," the boy answered, though it was clear from his expression he wished he had any excuse to say no.

The bishop motioned toward the nearest desk. "Why don't you sit down?"

"What's happened?" Jacob's eyes grew wild with fear, and his face became a sickish shade of gray. "They told me to sit down when they told me *Mamm* and *Daed* were dead. Is it *Onkel* Titus? Is he dead?"

Esther knew she should leave the answer to the bishop, but she couldn't bear the pain in the *kind*'s voice. Putting her arms around Jacob, she drew him close to her. He resisted for a moment, then clung to her as if she were a lifesaver in a turbulent sea.

"I'm sorry," she whispered against his hair.

"Danki." His voice was steadier than hers. As he stepped away and looked at Reuben and Nathaniel, he asked in his normal tone, "Can we go home now?"

"Go on out and turn the buggy around, so it'll be ready when we leave," Nathaniel said quietly.

The boy grabbed his hat, coat and lunch box before racing out of the schoolroom. Esther went to the window to watch him scurry to the buggy. He patted Bumper and spoke to him before climbing in and picking up the reins. Except for a brief moment when he'd held on to her, he acted as if nothing had occurred.

"We grieve in different ways," Reuben murmured, as if she'd spoken aloud. Turning to Nathaniel, he added, "You must watch for his moods to change abruptly. He understands more than most *kinder* his age about death and loss, but he's still only eight years old."

Walking away from the window, Esther asked, "What will happen to him now? Titus Fisher was, as far as we could find out, his only living relative."

"He's welcome to stay with me," Nathaniel replied quietly. "For as long as he needs to."

The tears that had scorched her eyes all day threatened to fall when she heard the genuine emotion in his words. Not only had Nathaniel made a positive change in Jacob, but the boy had done the same for him. Nathaniel had become more confident in handling the animals at the farm and had a clear vision of how he could make the farm a success.

If only he wasn't playing the field like Daniel, I could...

She silenced the thoughts. This was neither the time nor the place for them. She should be grateful she knew his intentions.

"That is *gut* of you, Nathaniel," Reuben said. "However, the choice isn't ours. With his *onkel*'s death, Jacob is now a ward of the Commonwealth of Pennsylvania. I received a call earlier today. An *Englisch* social worker named Chloe Lambert will be visiting you at your farm once the funeral is over."

"Is it just a formality?" Esther asked.

The bishop raked his fingers through his beard as he did often when he was distressed. "I wish I could say it was, but Nathaniel isn't related to Jacob, so there will need to be supervision by a social worker."

"What can we do?" Nathaniel asked.

"I'll be talking to the *Leit* about making a plan for taking care of the boy. I suggest you do the same. He has done well at your farm, Nathaniel." Reuben sighed and looked at Esther. "The two of you need to think about the ways you have helped the boy and ways you can in the future."

"We will," Esther said at the same time Nathaniel did. "Will that be enough to convince an *Englisch* social worker Jacob's place is here among us?"

The bishop looked steadily from her to Nathaniel. "We must heed the lesson in the Book of Proverbs. 'Trust in the Lord with all thine heart; and lean not unto thine own understanding. In all thy ways acknowledge Him, and He shall direct thy paths.' He knows what lies ahead and is here to guide us."

"What else can we do?"

She expected Reuben to answer, but instead Nathaniel did. "We must believe our combined efforts and prayer are enough to touch an *Englisch* woman's heart and open her eyes to the truth that Jacob's home is with us."

Chapter Fifteen

Esther closed the teacher's edition of the fifth graders' textbook. She rubbed her tired eyes and looked out at the star-strewn sky. It wasn't late, just after supper, but sunset was so early this time of year. As the weather grew colder, the stars became brighter and somehow felt closer to her window. She leaned back in her chair and turned out the propane light hissing on her bedroom table.

Instantly the sky seemed a richer black, and the stars burned more fiercely. She sat straighter when a shooting star raced across the sky. *Englischers* made wishes on them, but that was a *kind*'s game.

What would she wish if she believed in such silliness? For hearts to be healed, most especially Jacob's. The boy had been stoic during his *onkel*'s funeral, but she'd seen the anger in his eyes when he didn't think anyone was looking at him. He'd started getting into fights at school again and seemed to think everyone was against him. Nothing Esther said made a difference.

You should discuss this with Nathaniel. The thought had nagged her every day for the past week. She'd spoken with him a few times during the funeral, but otherwise she'd avoided him. It was cowardly, she knew, but allowing herself to be drawn to him again would be foolish. He wanted to play the field.

She heard her name shouted up the stairs. "Esther, a call came at the barn for you."

"For me?" She had no idea who'd use the phone to contact her.

Micah answered, "*Ja.* Jacob Fisher called. A cria is coming, and they could use your help."

Esther didn't hesitate. Jumping to her feet, she grabbed a thick wool shawl from the chest by her bed and picked up the bag of supplies she'd packed. She ran down the stairs, barely missing Micah who stood at the bottom.

"Jeremiah is getting your buggy ready," he said.

"Danki." She didn't add anything else as she raced into the kitchen, snatched her bonnet and set it on her head with one hand while opening the door with the other.

The ride to Nathaniel's farm seemed longer in the darkness. There wasn't much traffic, but she slowed at the crest of each hill in case a vehicle was coming. She wasn't worried solely about *Englisch* cars. Despite Alvin Lee's accident, others might foolishly be racing their buggies tonight.

She breathed a sigh of relief when she pulled into Nathaniel's farm lane. The house was dark, but light shone from the barn. She jumped from her buggy, collected her bag and ran in. She started to call out to Nathaniel and Jacob, but clamped her lips closed when she saw the astounding sight in front of her.

In the glow of several lanterns arranged around the barn, Nathaniel stood inside the alpacas' pen, his back to her. He was staring at Jacob. The boy was surrounded by the herd, which seemed to be seeking his attention. He stroked one, then another. None of them shied from his touch. His face was glowing with happiness.

She wanted to praise him for his patience in letting the alpacas come to him. She stayed silent because the sound of her voice might send the excitable creatures fleeing, and that could be dangerous for the one in labor.

Crossing the barn, she opened the gate so she could stand beside Nathaniel. He glanced at her with a wide grin before looking at the boy.

Jacob pushed his way through the herd and loped over to the gate. "Did you see that?"

"You're a *wunderbaar* friend to the alpacas," Esther said, then laughed when one of the braver ones trotted after him, clearly hoping he had something for her to eat. "They've discovered that."

"*Ja.* I like them, and they like me." His eyes glowed with joy.

"Well done," Nathaniel said, clapping his hand on the boy's shoulder with the respect one man showed another.

Esther looked at one corner of the pen where a young alpaca was lying on her side. Nathaniel started to give her a report on the alpaca's labor. She waved him to silence.

"Let the *mamm* alpaca do what she needs to," she said as she knelt in the hay by the gate.

"Shouldn't we do something?" asked Jacob.

"She should do well by herself. If she needs help, we'll be here to offer it. Otherwise, we'll watch and cheer when her cria comes."

"That's it?" asked Nathaniel.

"Alpacas have been giving birth on their own in the wild forever. She'll do fine."

Though Esther saw doubt on their faces, the alpaca proved her right when, about ten minutes later, the cria made its entrance, nose and front legs first. Within moments of its head's appearance, the cria was born. It sniffed the world, trying to find out more about it. The alpaca stretched to nose her newborn. A couple of the other alpacas came over to do the same, but she stood and got between them and her cria.

"Wait here," Esther whispered as she carried her bag closer to the *boppli.*

The *mamm* shied away, but not too far, her eyes remaining on the cria. Speaking in a low, steady voice, Esther opened the bag and withdrew a sling hooked to a handheld scale. She carefully lifted the unsteady cria into the sling and held it up.

"She's sixteen pounds," Esther said with a smile. "A *gut* size for a female cria." Lowering the *boppli* to the hay, she crooked a finger at Jacob. "Come over and see her."

"The *mamm* won't care?"

"They trust you now. Move slowly and don't get between her and the cria."

The boy crept closer. "She's cute."

"Would you like to pick out a name for her?" Nathaniel asked.

"Me?" His grin stretched his cheeks. "You want me to name the cria?"

"If you want to. Take a few days and think it over."

"Ja," Esther said. "Right now, the cria isn't going to do much other than eat and sleep. Her *mamm* will take

care of her, but in a few days, the cria will be running about and playing."

Jacob considered that, then asked, "What if something happens to her *mamm*?"

Esther wiped her hands on the towel Nathaniel held out to her. "She's healthy, and she should live a long time. Some live until they're twenty years old."

"My *mamm* wasn't much older when she died."

Esther couldn't move as she stared at the *kind* who was regarding her and Nathaniel with an acceptance beyond his years. Yet she saw the pain he was again trying to hide. Jacob seldom spoke of his parents and never this directly.

"We'll watch over the cria," she replied, "and we won't be the only ones. God keeps a loving eye on all of us."

"Not me."

Nathaniel started to say, "Of course He—"

Esther halted him. One thing she'd learned as a teacher and as an *aenti*, trying to tell *kinder* their feelings were wrong got her nowhere.

"Why do you think God doesn't look out for you?" she asked.

"Why would He? He knows how furious I am with Him. He let my *mamm* and *daed* die, and He let me live so I can't be with them."

Squatting in front of the *kind*, she put her hands on his shoulders. "We have to believe, no matter what happens, God loves us."

"But if He loved me, why…?" His voice cracked as tears filled his eyes that had been joyous moments before.

"Why did He take your parents? I can't give you an

answer, Jacob. There are things we can't know now. That's what faith is. Believing in God's *gut* and loving ways when our own hearts are broken."

"I miss them." He leaned into her, reforming his body to fit against hers.

"I know. I miss my *daed*, too."

Jacob raised his head. "You have your *mamm*."

"For which I'm grateful, but that doesn't lessen my sorrow when I think of my *daed* and how he used to make me laugh when I was a little girl." She wiped one of his tears away with the crook of her finger. "If he were here, he'd be in great pain, and I don't want him to suffer."

"My parents would have suffered, too. Really bad. *Onkel* Titus told me I shouldn't want them to stay here."

"It's okay to miss them and want to be with them."

"It is?"

"*Ja*, but we have to believe God has His reasons for healing some of us and for releasing others from their pain by bringing them home to Him. We have to see His grace either way and realize mere humans can't understand what He chooses. But we know God grieves along with us because He loves us."

"Does God cry, too?"

"When we turn away from Him," Nathaniel said. Pointing to the alpaca that had given birth, he added, "Look at her. She's glad because her *boppli* is alive. She wants to keep her cria close to her, to protect and nourish it. That's what makes her happy. Just as God is happy when we are close to Him."

"Oh." Jacob didn't say more as he watched the alpaca and the cria.

"When the cria is old enough to go off on her own,"

Esther whispered, "the alpaca won't be angry. She knows that is how life is intended to be, and to be angry at her daughter would be as useless as being angry at a piece of hay. That's how parents think, and God is our heavenly Father. He knows sometimes we have to make mistakes, but His love for us never falters. Even if you're angry with Him, He isn't angry with you."

The boy searched their faces, then looked at the alpacas. "He loves me like I love the alpacas." The tension slowly slid from his shoulders. Without another word, he went to the rest of the herd and let them surround him as he petted them.

Nathaniel smiled at Esther, and she saw the same pure happiness in his eyes as the boy's. It was a perfect moment.

And a moment was all it lasted. One moment, because before she could say anything, gravel crunched beneath rubber tires in the driveway. Someone was coming. Someone who wasn't driving in on metal wheels.

Her stomach cramped as the late model *Englisch* car stopped by the house and the driver turned off the engine. Through the windshield in the lights from the dashboard, she could see it was a young woman.

"The social worker." Esther didn't make it a question.

She heard the same uncertainty and dismay in his voice when he said, "We knew the state would be sending someone."

"But why now?"

Nathaniel glanced over his shoulder to where Jacob was relishing his chance to pet the alpacas and feed them by hand. Esther did the same. He knew what she was thinking. It'd been such a *wunderbaar* moment, and it was sad to have it interrupted by the outside world. But the outside world was there, and they must deal with it.

Putting his arm around Esther's shoulders and picking up a lantern, he told Jacob they'd be back in a few minutes. He wasn't sure if the boy heard them because he was enthralled by the alpacas nuzzling him.

The *Englisch* woman was stepping out of the car as they emerged from the barn. Chloe Lambert was nothing like he'd expected. Nothing like he'd feared. Instead of wearing a fancy business suit, the young woman had on khaki pants and a simple blouse. She wore sneakers like Esther's, and her dark hair was short and flattered her round face. One thing was as he'd anticipated. Chloe Lambert carried a briefcase with a long strap to allow it to hang from her shoulder.

"I'm Nathaniel Zook," he said.

She nodded and looked at Esther. "Where's Jacob Fisher?"

"He's feeding the alpacas. I'm Esther, by the way."

"Very nice to meet you, Esther. Is Jacob safe with those animals?"

Esther laughed, but the sound was laced with anxiety. "He's very safe. He's been trying to convince the herd for almost a month to let him get close to them. Tonight that happened just before a new one was born."

She glanced down at Esther's feet. "Is he wearing sneakers, too? Does he need to wear boots?"

"He's fine," Nathaniel said. "Why don't you come in and see for yourself?"

"Thank you. I'd like that." Chloe took a step, then looked steadily at them. "Please understand we want the same thing. What's best for the boy. I'm not your enemy or his."

Nathaniel nodded. "I'm sorry if we gave you that impression."

Miss Lambert smiled kindly. "You haven't. I wanted to make that clear. Now please show me where the boy is."

Esther began talking with the social worker as if they were longtime friends and with an ease Nathaniel couldn't have managed. He remembered the social workers who'd spoken with his parents at the hospital, outlining programs available to him and them. Some had sounded interesting and probably would have been approved by their bishop, but his parents wanted nothing more to do with *Englischers* and hospitals and *doktors* and tests.

Had they been right to distrust the *Englisch* system, or had it been only the unrelenting fear and guilt driving them? He hadn't known then, and he didn't know now. At last he understood how intrusive it was to have someone examining every aspect of his life and how little control he had over the situation.

I can hand control over to You, Lord, and trust You'll direct our paths in a direction where we can travel toward You together.

The prayer eased the initial panic he hadn't been able to submerge. No wonder Miss Lambert thought he saw her as an enemy. As he watched Esther introducing Miss Lambert to Jacob and listened while the social worker spoke to the boy about the alpacas as if they were the most important thing in the world, he relaxed further. He doubted the social worker was as interested in the herd as she acted, but she was allowing Jacob to tell her every detail about the cria's birth. She oohed and aahed over the adorable *boppli*. It was a *gut* way for her to get insight into the boy's life.

A half hour later, they were sitting in Nathaniel's living room. Miss Lambert got out her computer and put it on a chair she'd drawn near where she sat.

"Do you mind?" she asked as she opened her laptop. "I'd like to take notes while we're talking. It'll make it easier for me later to transfer the information to the department's forms."

"Of course not," Nathaniel replied. What else could he say? He hated everything about this situation where each word he spoke could be the wrong one. *Lord, be with us today and guide our words and actions so Miss Lambert sees Jacob belongs here with this community. Here with me!* The last came directly from his heart.

"Let me say again how much I appreciate you being willing to let me come and visit like this, Mr. Zook."

"Please call me Nathaniel."

"Thank you. I appreciate that, and I think it'll be simpler if you call me Chloe."

"*Danki.* I mean, thank you."

She smiled, obviously trying to put them at ease. "I understand enough of the language of the plain folk to know what *danki* means. I've worked with other plain families, which is why I was assigned as Jacob's social worker. If you say something I don't understand, I'll ask you to explain. Please do the same if I say something you don't understand."

Nathaniel nodded and watched Esther do the same. Jacob was hunched on his chair, trying to make himself as small as possible. Did he have any idea why the social worker was there? Probably not. It was more likely he wanted to return to the alpacas.

Chloe looked at Esther. "I understand you are Jacob's teacher."

"I am."

She typed a few keys on her computer, then said, "I know it'll be an imposition, but I'll need to see Jacob at school. I can't let you know before I arrive." She gave Esther a wry smile. "We're supposed to drop in so we see what's really going on. I hope that won't be a problem."

"The scholars—our students are accustomed to having parents come to the school to help. You're welcome to come anytime you need to, but I must ask you not to talk to the *kinder* without their parents' permission."

"That is fair. Will you arrange for me to obtain the permission if I need it?"

"It will be for the best if our bishop does."

"That's Reuben Lapp, right?"

"Ja."

Chloe smiled as she continued typing. "I've already spoken with Bishop Lapp. He expressed his concerns about the situation, and I told him—as I'm telling you—those concerns will be taken into consideration before any decision will be made."

"Gut." Relief was evident in Esther's voice.

When she looked at him, Nathaniel gave her what he hoped she'd see as a bolstering smile. The situation between them might be tenuous now, but she was his greatest ally...as she'd always been. It wasn't a *kind*'s game they were caught up in now, but he knew he could trust she'd be there for him and for Jacob. Her heart was steadfast, and in spite of her trepidation now, he knew she had the courage of the Old Testament woman whose name she shared. That Esther had done all she could to save her people, and Esther Stoltzfus would do no less for an orphaned boy.

His attention was pulled back to the social worker when Chloe said, "Now, Nathaniel, I've got a few questions for you."

When she saw Nathaniel's shoulders stiffen, Esther wanted to put her hand out to him as she had in the schoolroom on the day they'd told Jacob of his *onkel*'s passing. She wasn't sure how Chloe would react, so she clasped her fingers together on her lap.

She listened to questions about Jacob's schedule, what he ate, and where he slept. The boy began to squirm with boredom, and she asked if he could be excused. Her respect for the *Englisch* woman rose when Chloe gave him a warm smile and told him to enjoy his time with the alpacas, but not to spend so much time with them he didn't get his homework done.

"I don't give the *kinder* homework," Esther said when Jacob regarded the social worker with bafflement. "They've got chores, so the scholars complete their work at school. Besides, they need some time to play and be *kinder*."

Chloe's smile broadened as Jacob made his escape. "I wish more people felt that way. Children need to be children, but too many find themselves in situations where that's impossible." She looked at Nathaniel. "Just a few more questions. I know this must seem like the whole world poking its nose into your business, but we must be certain being here is the best place for Jacob."

"It is." Not a hint of doubt was in his voice or on his face.

"I hope you're right." Glancing at the screen, she asked, "Do you have family in the area, Nathaniel?"

"Not any longer. This farm belonged to my grandparents, and when they died, it became mine."

"So your parents are deceased, too?"

"No. They're in Indiana with my four sisters and younger brother. Two of my sisters are married, and I have several nephews and nieces. They live near my parents."

"So there's nobody here to help you with Jacob?"

"Our community is here to help if we need it." His smile was so tight it looked painful. "So far, we haven't. Jacob and I have gotten along well."

As she'd promised, the social worker had only a few more questions. Esther listened as Nathaniel answered thoughtfully and without hesitation or evasion. When Chloe asked to see the boy's room, Esther didn't follow them upstairs. She remained in the living room, listening to the hiss of the propane lamp and staring at the computer. If she peeked at the screen, would she be able to see what Chloe had written?

She couldn't do that. If the social worker found her snooping, it might be a mark against Nathaniel. What did Chloe think about Jacob's situation? Would she recommend he stay with Nathaniel?

The social worker and Nathaniel returned to the lower floor. They spoke easily before Nathaniel said he'd go and get Jacob to have a few words with the social worker.

As he went outside, Chloe closed her computer and put it in her bag. "Thank you for taking time to speak with me." She straightened. "I appreciate you being forthcoming. Some people aren't, but you and your husband—"

"Nathaniel isn't my husband."

The social worker stared at her, astonished. "I'm sorry. When I saw you together, I assumed you were married. I know I shouldn't assume anything about anyone, but you two seem like a perfectly matched set..." She turned away, embarrassed.

"Would it make a difference in your recommendation for where Jacob will live?" Esther asked before she could halt herself.

"What?" Chloe faced her.

"If Nathaniel and I were married?"

"Maybe. Maybe not. I can't give you a definite answer. Without any blood relationship between either of you and the boy, it's far more complicated."

"Jacob having a *mamm* and a *daed*..." She halted and amended, "Having a mother and a father would make a difference, wouldn't it?"

"It could." The social worker put the bag's strap over her shoulder. "Don't worry that my mistake will have any impact on this case, Esther. I can see both of you care deeply about the boy. However, sometimes the best thing for a child isn't what the adults around him want. We have to think first and foremost of what will give him the stable home he's never had. We prefer that to be with two parents."

Esther felt her insides turn to ice. She couldn't doubt Chloe's earnestness, but were her words a warning the state would take Jacob away? Somehow she managed to choke out a goodbye as the social worker left to speak to Jacob once more.

Groping for a chair, she sat and stared at the spot where Jacob had been curled up. She didn't move and couldn't think of anything other than watching the boy being taken away from his community and his heritage.

She wasn't sure how long she sat there before Nathaniel returned. He strode into the living room. When she turned her gaze toward him, his face grew grayer.

"What is it?" he asked. "Did she say something to you?"

She explained the short conversation before saying, "Chloe suggested her superiors would prefer Jacob being in a family with two parents who can help him try to overcome the pain he has suffered. We can't offer him that now unless..."

"It sounds as if you want me to ask you to be my wife."

"I don't know what I'm saying, Nathaniel." She surged to her feet. "All I know for sure is Jacob needs to stay here. He's begun to heal, and if he's taken away, he'll lose any progress he's made."

"Did you tell her that?"

"No." Her eyes swam in tears. "I don't think I needed to. She looked dismayed when she found out we aren't married."

"Esther, you're probably the best friend I've ever had. Now and when we were kids, but—"

"That's all we'll ever be." Why did the words taste bitter? She'd told him many times friendship was what she wanted from him. She'd been lying. Not just to him, but to herself. Maybe not at the beginning when she first learned he'd come back to Paradise Springs, but as the days went on and she spent time with him and Jacob. Sometime, during those weeks in spite of her assertions, she'd begun to believe she and Nathaniel might be able to build a life together.

Then he'd kissed her…and her old fears of taking a risk had returned.

His broad hands framed her face and tilted it toward him so his gaze met hers. She saw his sorrow. Did he regret their agreement to be friends, too? Or was his grief focused on Jacob?

"I can't marry you, Esther. Not now." His voice broke. "Not ever."

She pulled away before her tears fell and betrayed her. "*Danki* for telling me that. You've made yourself really clear."

"Esther, wait!" he called as she started to walk away. "I've got a *gut* reason for saying that. I should have told you this right from the beginning, but I was ashamed."

"Of what? Most young men like to play the field, as you put it so tersely."

"What?"

"I heard you and Micah and Daniel laughing at the wedding about how you weren't going to settle down."

"Esther, look at me."

She slowly faced him. "Don't tell me you didn't say that, because I heard you."

"I'm sure you did. What you didn't hear were the words before those. Micah and I were teasing Daniel about his habits of bringing a different girl home from every event. I was repeating his words to him in jest."

"If that's not the reason—"

"The truth is I may never be able to be a *daed*." The resignation in his voice was vivid on his face. It was the expression of a man who had fought long and hard for a goal, but it was still beyond his reach, and it might be forever.

"I don't understand," she whispered.

"After we left Paradise Springs, I came back the next summer."

"I remember." She did. That year she'd been too bold and told him she planned to marry him. How ironic that sounded now!

"I didn't return the next summer because I was ill." He took a deep breath and said, "I had leukemia."

"Cancer?" she choked out. "I never knew."

"I know. My parents wanted to keep it quiet, even from our neighbors in Indiana. They sold off most of their farmland to pay the bills for my treatment." He rubbed his hands together as if he didn't know what else to do with them. "They were horrified one of their children was weak enough to succumb to such a disease."

"Weakness or strength has nothing to do with it." She pulled his hands apart, folding one between hers. "You know that, don't you?"

"*I* do, but I don't think they've ever accepted the truth. They always believed they or I had done something wrong. Something to call the scourge down on me." His mouth tightened into a straight line. "That's what they call it. The scourge."

"I'm sorry." She was beginning to understand his compassion for Jacob and why it went beyond the simple kindness of helping a *kind* who was alone in the world. He knew too well how it was to be different.

"I appreciate that, Esther."

"You are all right now?"

"As *gut* as if I'd never had cancer. With chemotherapy and radiation, the *Englisch doktors* saved my life from the disease. That's how they saw it. A disease that strikes indiscriminately, not a scourge sent to punish my family." He sighed. "However, the *Englisch doktors* warned me that the treatments probably had made it impossible for me ever to father a *boppli*."

Tears flooding her eyes blurred his face, but she doubted she'd ever be able to erase his desolate expression from her memory.

"Oh, Nathaniel, I'm sorry. I know how you love *kinder*." She pressed her hands over her heart. "Now you have to worry about losing Jacob. If you think it'll make a difference—"

"Don't say it, Esther. I won't do that to you. I won't ask you to take the risk. How many times have you told me you aren't the same person you were when we were little? That you like to consider all aspects of an issue before you make a decision, that you no longer leap before you look around you."

"Nathaniel—"

"No, Esther, I'm sure of this. I've seen you with your scholars. You love *kinder*. You light up when they're around, whether at school or at home with your nieces and nephews. Or with Jacob who, despite his grumbling, appreciates the time you spend with him."

"So I have nothing to say about this?"

"What do you mean?"

She stood on tiptoe and pressed her lips against his. When his arms came around her, they didn't enfold her. They drew her away but not before she saw the regret in his eyes.

"Stop it, Esther. My *daed* warned me I must be stronger than I was when I contracted cancer." He groaned. "I never imagined I'd have to be this strong and push you away."

"Your *daed* is wrong." She took his hand again and folded it between her fingers as if in prayer. "I was wrong, Nathaniel, when I let myself believe it's a *gut* idea to hide from my adult pain by putting aside my childhood love of adventure. Remember what it was like then? We never questioned if something was worth the risk. We simply went with our hearts."

"And ended up bruised and battered."

"And happy." She hesitated, then realized if she hoped for him to open his heart to her, she must be willing to do the same to him. With a tentative smile, she said, "Well, except for one time I've never forgotten."

"Which time?"

"You don't remember?" She was astonished.

"I'm not sure what you're referring to. We got into a lot of scrapes together, so you'll need to be more specific."

She looked down at their hands. "I'm talking about the day when you were visiting from Indiana and I came over to your grandparents' farm, and I took your hand… like this."

He smiled as he put one finger under her chin and tipped it so her gaze met his. "I do remember. I thought you were the most *wunderbaar* girl I'd ever known." He chuckled. "That hasn't changed."

"I told you I was going to marry you as soon as we were old enough. Remember that?"

"*Ja*. I thought you were joking."

"*I* thought I was going to die of embarrassment."

He put his hands on her shoulders and smiled. "Never be embarrassed, Esther, to tell someone how you feel. You were brave enough to be honest. If more of us were like that, the world would be a better place."

"It didn't feel like that at the time." She took a deep breath, knowing if she backed away from risking her heart now, she'd never be able to risk it again. "I'm not going to be embarrassed now when I tell you I love you. I always have, and I always will. Get that through your thick head, Nathaniel Zook. I love you. Not some *kinder* we might be blessed with some day. You. I'm not saying this because of Jacob. I'm saying this because I can't keep the truth to myself any longer. If you don't love me, tell me, but don't push me away because you're trying to protect me from what God has planned for the future."

She held her breath as he stared at her. Had she been too blunt? Had she pushed too hard?

"That was quite a speech," he said with a grin.

"Don't ask me to repeat it."

"Not even the part when you said you love me?" His arm around her waist drew her to him. As he bent toward her, he whispered, "I want to hear you repeat that every day of our lives, and I'll tell you how much I've always loved you, Esther Stoltzfus. I don't need to be like your brother and play the field." He chuckled. "Actually I was in the outfield when you tumbled into my arms. From that moment, I knew it was where I wanted you always to be. But—"

She put her finger to his lips. "Let's leave our future in God's hands."

"As long as you're in mine." He captured her lips, and she softened against him.

Savoring his kiss and combing her fingers through his thick hair, letting its silk sift between her fingers, she wondered why she'd resisted telling him the truth until now. Some things were worth any amount of risk.

Epilogue

"Hurry, hurry!" called Chloe as she motioned for them to enter a small room beside one of the fancy courtrooms. "You should have been here ten minutes ago so we could review everything before we go before the judge."

"We're sorry. We were delayed." Nathaniel, dressed in his church Sunday *mutze* and white shirt, smiled at Esther. In fact, he hadn't stopped smiling the whole time they rode in Gerry's van from Paradise Springs into the city of Lancaster.

She put her hand on his arm, still a bit unsteady after her bout of sickness that morning. When it first had afflicted her last week, she'd thought she'd contracted some bug. However, the illness came only in the first couple of hours of each morning before easing to a general queasiness the rest of the day. It had continued day after day for nearly ten days now.

This morning, she'd told Nathaniel she believed she was pregnant. His shock had been endearing. She'd warned him that she must go to the midwife and have a test to confirm her pregnancy tomorrow, but she was certain what the test would show. They'd been married only three months, taking their vows barely a month after Ezra and Leah had, and already God had blessed them with a *boppli*.

"As long as you're here now." Chloe smiled at them. "Any questions before we go in?"

Jacob tugged on Nathaniel's sleeve. When Nathaniel bent down, the boy whispered frantically in his ear.

The social worker smiled and answered before Nathaniel spoke. "Down the hall on your right. Don't forget to wash your hands, Jacob. The judge will want to shake your hand when she finalizes your adoption."

As the boy scurried away, Nathaniel put his arm around Esther. They listened while Chloe explained again what would happen when they went into the courtroom. Official paperwork and recommendations from social services would be presented to the judge, who'd already reviewed copies of them. The judge might ask Jacob a few questions, but the procedure was simple and quick.

Jacob rushed into the room as another door opened, and a woman invited them into the courtroom. As they walked in, Jacob took Nathaniel's hand and then Esther's. They went together to a table where they sat facing a lady judge on her high seat behind a sign that read Judge Eloise Probert.

The paperwork was placed in front of the judge who barely glanced at it. She smiled at Jacob and asked him if he understood what was going on.

"*Ja...* I mean, yes, your honor," he replied as he'd been instructed. "Once you say so, I won't be Jacob Fisher any longer. I'll be Jacob Zook, and Nathaniel and

Esther will be my new *daed* and *mamm*." He gulped. "I mean, dad and mom."

"That's right, Jacob." Judge Probert had a nice smile and a gentle voice. "So this is what you want? To be Nathaniel and Esther's son?"

Jacob nodded so hard Esther had to bite her lip not to laugh. She heard a smothered sound from either side of her and saw Nathaniel and Chloe trying not to laugh, too.

"More than anything else in the whole world," Jacob answered. "Except maybe a couple more alpacas for our herd."

This time, nobody restrained their laughter, including the judge. "Well, I'll leave that decision to your new parents. Congratulations, Zook family. From this day forward, you *are* a forever family. All three of you."

Esther hugged Jacob and Nathaniel at the same time. She felt so happy and blessed.

After the paperwork was checked and they signed a few more papers and shook the judge's hand as well as Chloe's, Esther walked out of the courtroom with her husband and their son. They smiled at other families awaiting their turn to go before the judge. Congratulations were called to them, and her face hurt from smiling so widely.

They stepped through the doors and walked toward the tall columns edging the front of the courthouse, Nathaniel said, "You know, the judge got almost everything right."

"Almost?" she asked.

"She said the three of us are a forever family. It's the *four* of us."

Tapping his nose, she said, "So far. Who knows how often God will bless us?"

With a laugh, he spun her into his arms and kissed her soundly. Then, each of them grabbing one of Jacob's hands, they walked toward where the white van was parked. The van that would take their family home.

* * * * *

Don't miss these other AMISH HEARTS *stories from Jo Ann Brown:*

AMISH HOMECOMING
AN AMISH MATCH

Find more great reads at www.LoveInspired.com

Dear Reader,

Life is busy. It pulls us this way and that. Sometimes it pulls us away from the people who are very important in our lives. If those people's paths intersect with ours again, it's a special blessing. The story of two people who reconnect after ten years apart and have a second chance at love—a grown-up chance, this time—was a story I wanted to explore in this book. It was fun to discover how much these people still had in common and how much they needed to learn about each other. I hope you agree their happy-ever-after was worth the effort.

Stop in and visit me at www.joannbrownbooks.com. Look for my next story in the Amish Hearts series, "A Christmas to Remember" coming in this year's Christmas anthology *Amish Christmas Blessings* from Love Inspired.

Wishing you many blessings,
Jo Ann Brown

COMING NEXT MONTH FROM
Love Inspired®

Available September 20, 2016

THE RANCHER'S TEXAS MATCH
Lone Star Cowboy League: Boys Ranch
by Brenda Minton
Rancher Tanner Barstow knows Macy Swanson is only in Haven, Texas, to claim guardianship of her nephew. But can he convince the city girl to give small-town life—and him—a chance?

LONE STAR DAD
The Buchanons • by Linda Goodnight
Gena Satterfield is surprised when her solitary neighbor Quinn Buchanon starts bonding with her rebellious nephew. He's got a way with the boy—and with her heart—but the secret she's hiding may just tear them apart forever.

LOVING ISAAC
Lancaster County Weddings • by Rebecca Kertz
Isaac Lapp is looking to make amends for the mistakes of his past. Having once abandoned her for the *Englisch* life, can he convince his long-ago friend Ellen Mast of his promise...and of his love?

HOMETOWN HOLIDAY REUNION
Oaks Crossing • by Mia Ross
In town to temporarily run the family business, Cam Stewart begins to reconsider his stay when he reconnects with Erin Kinsley. His best friend's little sister has grown into a lovely woman—one he hopes to make a part of his permanent family.

A TEMPORARY COURTSHIP
Maple Springs • by Jenna Mindel
A chance at a coveted promotion has Darren Zelinsky teaching a class in Bay Willows, where he instantly becomes smitten with Bree Anderson. The charming musician will soon be heading west, unless the hometown boy can show her that her future lies with him.

A FAMILY FOR THE FARMER
by Laurel Blount
Farmer Abel Whitlock is determined to help single mom Emily Elliot run Goosefeather Farm. If she fails, he'll inherit. But he has no interest in claiming the land—he's after claiming his longtime crush's heart.

LOOK FOR THESE AND OTHER LOVE INSPIRED BOOKS WHEREVER BOOKS ARE SOLD, INCLUDING MOST BOOKSTORES, SUPERMARKETS, DISCOUNT STORES AND DRUGSTORES.

LICNM0916

REQUEST YOUR FREE BOOKS!

2 FREE INSPIRATIONAL NOVELS
PLUS 2
FREE
MYSTERY GIFTS

SPECIAL EXCERPT FROM

Love Inspired

*When Macy Swanson must suddenly raise her young
nephew, help comes in the form of single rancher and
boys ranch volunteer Tanner Barstow. Can he help her
see she's mom—and rural Texas—material?*

Read on for a sneak preview of the first book in the
LONE STAR COWBOY LEAGUE: BOYS RANCH
*miniseries, THE RANCHER'S TEXAS MATCH
by Brenda Minton.*

She leaned back in the seat and covered her face with her
hands. "I am angry. I'm mad because I don't know what to
do for Colby. And the person I always went to for advice
is gone. Grant is gone. I think Colby and I were both in
a delusional state, thinking they would come home. But
they're not. I'm not getting my brother, my best friend,
back. Colby isn't getting his parents back. And it isn't
fair. It isn't fair that I had to—"

Her eyes closed, and she shook her head.

"Macy?"

She pinched the bridge of her nose. "No. I'm not going
to say that. I lost a job and gave up an apartment. Colby
lost his parents. What I lost doesn't amount to anything. I
lost things I don't miss."

"I think you're wrong. I think you miss your life.
There's nothing wrong with that. Accept it, or it'll eat
you up."

Tanner pulled up to her house.

"I miss my life." She said it on a sigh. "I wouldn't be anywhere else. But I have to admit, there are days I wonder if Colby would be better off with someone else, with anyone but me. But I'm his family. We have each other."

"Yes, and in the end, that matters."

"But…" She bit down on her lip and glanced away from him, not finishing.

"But what?"

"What if I'm not a mom? What if I can't do this?" She looked young sitting next to him, her green eyes troubled.

"I'm guessing that even a mom who planned on having a child would still question if she could do it."

She reached for the door. "Thank you for letting me talk about Colby."

"Anytime." He said it, and then he realized the door that had opened.

She laughed. "Don't worry. I won't be calling at midnight to talk about my feelings."

"If you did, I'd answer."

She stood on tiptoe and touched his cheek to bring it down to her level. When she kissed him, he felt floored by the unexpected gesture. Macy had soft hair, soft gestures and a soft heart. She was easy to like. He guessed if a man wasn't careful, he'd find himself falling a little in love with her.

Don't miss
THE RANCHER'S TEXAS MATCH by Brenda Minton,
available October 2016 wherever
Love Inspired® books and ebooks are sold.

www.LoveInspired.com

*Sheriff Shane Timmons just wants to be left alone,
but this Christmas he'll find that family is what he's
always been looking for.*

Read on for an excerpt from
THE SHERIFF'S CHRISTMAS TWINS,
the next heartwarming book in the
SMOKY MOUNTAIN MATCHES series.

"We have a situation at the mercantile, Sheriff."

Shane Timmons reached for his gun belt.

The banker held up his hand. "You won't be needing
that. This matter requires finesse, not force."

"What's happened?"

"I suggest you come see for yourself."

Shane's curiosity grew as he followed Claude outside
into the crisp December day and continued on to the
mercantile. Half a dozen trunks were piled beside the
entrance. Unease pulled his shoulder blades together.
His visitors weren't due for three more days. He did a
quick scan of the street, relieved there was no sign of the
stagecoach.

Claude held the door and waited for him to enter first.
The pungent stench of paint punched him in the chest.
His gaze landed on a knot of men and women in the far
corner.

"Why didn't you watch where you were going? Where
are your parents?"

"I—I'm terribly sorry, ma'am" came the subdued reply. "My ma's at the café."

"This is what happens when children are allowed to roam through the town unsupervised."

Shane rounded the aisle and wove his way through the customers, stopping short at the sight of statuesque, matronly Gertrude Messinger, a longtime Gatlinburg resident and wife of one of the gristmill owners, doused in green liquid. While her upper half remained untouched, her full skirts and boots were streaked and splotched with paint. Beside her, ashen and bug-eyed, stood thirteen-year-old Eliza Smith.

"Quinn Darling." Gertrude's voice boomed with outrage. "I expect you to assign the cost of a new dress to the Smiths' account."

At that, Eliza's freckles stood out in stark contrast to her skin.

"One moment, if you will, Mr. Darling," a third person chimed in. "The fault is mine, not Eliza's."

The voice put him in mind of snow angels and piano recitals and cookies swiped from silver platters. But it couldn't belong to Allison Ashworth. She and her brother, George, wouldn't arrive until Friday. Seventy-two more hours until his past collided with his present.

He wasn't ready.